Silly Sixteen

Octavia Ann Davis

Order this book online at www.trafford.com
or email orders@trafford.com

Most Trafford titles are also available at major online book retailers.

Printed in the United States of America.

ISBN: 978-1-4907-1633-6 (sc)
ISBN: 978-1-4907-1632-9 (e)

Trafford rev. 10/24/2013

www.trafford.com
North America & international
toll-free: 1 888 232 4444 (USA & Canada)
fax: 812 355 4082

To My Readers

"ALL" Young Women
Brittney Scott
&
Deborah Johnson

"It's important a girl
knows her value."

Book is dedicated to all the special
Girls in the world.

Table of Contents

Chapter One

Oh my God, it's the middle of the night and this phone is ringing sooooo super loud. Half asleep, I read five a.m. backwards on the alarm clock. Thank God my mother is sleep. "Hello, I answered with a raspy voice." "Hello, may I speak to Tiffany please?" "Speaking, who is this?" I asked. "It's me, Anthony". "What's wrong and why are you calling here so late Anthony?" He paused without answering. "Umm, when was the last time you talk to Darius?" "Last night, why?" I asked. "Look, I know it's late and everything but I need to get in touch with him. I mean, I can't wait another night. Tiff, do you know that nigga owe me money? I'm sitting here in college broke as hell because he is dodging my phone calls and shit. I can't even pay my phone bill. I'm on my home boy cell phone right now. Darius is not answering his phone and I guess he thinks if he keeps dodging me that he won't have to pay me my money back. You tell your boyfriend or better yet, my so call best friend to get his shit together." "Anthony it's late, I will give him a call tomorrow." As soon as I hung up my alarm went off for school.

It was the end of the summer and the beginning of a new school year in Tampa, Florida. This year I'm a proud high school senior. I walked to my 4th period British Literature class and spoke to a few folks from last year, then went to the back of the class with my girl Kayla. "Hey girl what's up," she said with a smile. We're seniors this year and girl I can't wait until homecoming. So what's up girl, that's a tight outfit but you know I look better in it, right Tiff?" "Shut up fool," I said as we hugged one another before taking our seats. "Kayla what's going on with Te-Te and that chump she creeping with?" "Tiff girl let me tell you, Te-Te is now eight months pregnant and you know she's due at the end of September. Carlos punk ass talking about they should move in together." "WHAT, she's only seventeen," I said choking off the apple juice I was drinking. Kayla continued, "Yeah girl, they talking about moving in together between now and Thanksgiving." "Yeah, well, we will see how long that last," I said in such disbelief. "You know what Tiff, what make it so bad is she knows he's not about nothing. She just can't seem to look pass him because she's having his baby". Kayla continued, "Te-Te was at his mother's house for a dinner party and Carlos never showed up until 11p.m. that night. She called me on the phone the next day crying. So I asked her where he said he was at and she told me outside at his homeboy's barbeque. She said Carlos forgot his mom was having a dinner party. I guess girlfriend was so busy worrying about him that she forgot it poured down raining on Valentine's Day."

I decided to change the subject. "So anyway did you find out about our senior fees because I seriously need a job?" "Yeah Tiff, our dues are five hundred and eight dollars." After she told me the cost of the dues, my stomach turned upside down. Our teacher was running very late, (for whatever reason) so I laid my head on the desk for the next thirty minutes until the dismissal bell rung.

I got up to stretch then begin walking towards the class room door. I turned around as Kayla followed behind me and whispered in her ear. "I heard about you girl but I haven't told anybody yet. Just know that I know and word is spreading around school fast. Slow yourself down," I said then walked ahead. A month of school quickly passed by and a job was desperately needed to my pay senior dues. I've spent most of my weekends and free time looking for work that would fit my school schedule. I was tired of watching my mother work like a dog every day to pay off bills in the house and have absolutely nothing left over for her. Today I came home early from my job search because my feet were hurting. Due to the phone constantly ringing, I couldn't concentrate on my math homework.

"Ma", I yelled from the crack of my bedroom door. The phone rang again. "Ma, can you get it for me?" "I'm trying to bake some fish and cook dinner. It's probably one of those nappy headed kids calling for you anyway," She yells from the kitchen. I answered the phone in frustration. "Hello!!!!!" "Yeah what's up," the familiar voice said. "Nothing, why are you calling now," I said as if he should have called some time ago. "What you talking about baby?" "Darius, you didn't call me Thursday, Friday, or Saturday." "I was with my cousin and spending time with family." "You must think I'm stuck on dumb boy. You couldn't pick one hour out of twenty-four hours for three days in a row to call me Darius?" "I'm sorry Tiff. Look outside your bedroom window." I looked outside my window and saw him in his car riding pass with three other guys in the car with him. "I was about to come see you, but I see your mom's car is outside" he said. "I don't see how you thought you were coming to visit with other guys in the car. Sounds like a bunch of bull Darius." "I'm going to call you back later, okay, Tiff?" "Yeah whatever," I said with a frustrated tone of voice. "I love you," Darius oddly said. I didn't say it back because he sounded suspicious. So I told him goodbye and hung up the phone. Five minutes passed before I realize he hasn't said I love you in a very long time. So I called him back and asked him what he's been doing all day. "Darius?" "What's up he answered?" "Darius who you been with because you're guilty of something." "Why you say that?" "Do you know how long it's been since I heard you say I love you?" "Aight then, I won't say it anymore."

"Whatever your missing the point and another thing how come you're not answering Anthony's phone calls?" "I already told him I'm gonna send him his money and to not rush me." "Okay but you know you're wrong though. You know he don't have money and he's in college broke so why would you borrow money you can't pay back? As a matter of fact Darius you've been neglecting a whole lot of people lately. Don't call me back until you call Anthony and get it together." "Aight then, he said with ease then hung up in my face. I was so upset that I pulled out some paper and decided to lay across my bed to write.

Dear diary, I need to be honest with myself because I'm tired of being blinded by love. For some reason something deep inside of me will not trust my boyfriend. I love him to death because he is the only one I ever been with sexually and I plan on keeping it that way. But . . . . I often wonder if he has ever cheated on me or is he with another girl from time to time. Sometimes I wonder if I should have just listened to my mother a long time ago and left him alone. I closed my diary and went to sleep. The next day I came home from school and continued to write in my diary on the kitchen table. Dear diary, he's mad at me now because I told him not to call me until he call Anthony back. I haven't heard from him since yesterday and days like yesterday and today make feel as though he's a cheater. This fool has made no attempt to call me back and it shows lack of effort. What happened with this relationship? This relationship was the best in the world in my eyes. I wonder if it ran its course because I'm not the same person anymore and neither is he. I got up from the front room table to wash the dishes my mother screamed for me to do thirty minutes ago. I then sat on my couch and turned on a gospel cd. I couldn't help the tears from falling down my face. For some reason it seem like ever since I've been with my boyfriend, I've been distracted. I have taken my focus off GOD. Lately, I've been backsliding so fast that I'm ashamed to look in the mirror. People say I'm beautiful but inside I feel ugly and I believe I always will be ugly until I fix myself spiritually. Some nights guilt takes over me because I know committing fornication is just as worst as killing someone. The bible says no sin is greater than another (James 2:10). In God's eyes sin is sin and it doesn't matter how big or small the sin is. I often ask myself, why am I having sex with my boyfriend because it dam sure aint because I love him. Being young minded, I believe it was insecurity. The thought of *If I don't then somebody else will.* What stupid thinking I had because the truth is . . . . YES, there are several females who are willing to have sex but how many can you find who are willing to wait for marriage? Real value is buried deep within those girls. **Any girl** can possess that value. All they have to do is **choose it** and choose to be different. And . . . . If I never conquer it then it will continue to conquer me

When I was a virgin, my friends kept telling me how great sex felt. At that particular time in my life, I was a proud virgin and I secretly believe some of my so called girl friends over exaggerated their sexual experience because they are jealous of me being a virgin. Eventually, going into my senior year of high school, curiosity killed the cat. I became weak when I stopped focusing on God's word. I really felt like I was ready and lost my virginity a month before I turned seventeen. I didn't give my virginity because I was proving to love him. Hell no, that would be even dumber than the reason why I actually did it. I gave it because my mother hated him and I just wanted him to have a piece of me forever no matter what she thought. I now realize that was a dumb ass decision but I swear back then it just felt so real. My mother did everything in her power to separate us instead of asking me why I like the boy so I rebelled. I felt like she was making a decision for me without trusting me to make a decision on my own. She was always trying to restrict me in my every move. I didn't even want to have sex with the boy. It's something about strict parents that makes you want to do the exact opposite. Sad to say . . . . the truth is . . . . I gave my virginity to Darius in order to prove a point to my mother. It had nothing to do with me being so deeply in love and all that other crazy shit you see on TV. BUT AT THE END OF THE DAY IT WAS STILL STUPID!!!

A young lady's virginity is truly one of those things you can't get back once it's gone. I'm not sad about it, I just wish I waited. My relationship with Darius was on the down low for a while because my mother didn't want me near him. She thought he was bad company for me and it doesn't take a rocket scientist to figure out why she felt that way. She didn't like him because of what I regretfully told her about him. Darius was the first boy I ever got serious with and I wanted to share every secret I had with my mother (huge fucking mistake). My mother and I always had close relationships to be able to talk about anything and I do mean *anything*. So, I figure since she was once a teenager and been through similar situations, why not ask her for advice. Darius use to be a huge car thief and just a thief in general (I later found out). So I told her all of his business from his past, but I also told her, he changed. She didn't want to believe the "He changed part".

So she did everything in her will to keep me away from him. She said she was doing it for my good and she didn't want to see me broken hearted over a low life fool who doesn't think highly of himself. But to me, her telling me that I couldn't see him again was breaking my heart. When I asked to go out with him, my mother would change into Cinderella's step mother, which led to arguing. So for the past five months our relationship has been on the down low (THE DL) from my mother. I'll tell you one thing though, my mother don't lie when it comes to things she know or either been through. I now regret being in a relationship with Darius because I often have to lie about what I'm doing and where I'm going. It hurts me to do so but I'm in so deep that I can't find my way out. I feel like GOD is angry with me because I'm sinning when I absolutely know better. Guilt is why I stop praying. I feel like. Sometimes I wonder if I lost my soul over love that's not even true. In vain, every time I go back to GOD, I seem to backslide and disappoint both him and myself over again. So I've gotten to the point of not even trying. The devil is always on the mission to find your weakness so he can to use it against the treasures of your heart. In my case God was my treasure. After writing my heart out I did something I haven't done in months. I prayed. Then a thought came to my brain. If I was perfect and could fix my own flaws, I wouldn't need God. Since I'm not perfect I need him regardless if I'm in sin or not. All God wants at the end of the day, is for YOU TO GO TO HIM and forget about what you've done (Matthew 11:28).

Chapter Two

My phone has been ringing all night and I know it's my boyfriend. My mother is at work as usual at this time, which is why he's been calling me back to back. I don't know who he thinks he is. He hasn't called me so he's going to wait before I answer the phone for him. Ring, ring, ring, ring, ring, ring, ring, ring, ring. I wish he stop calling me. Ring, ring, ring, ring, ring . . . .

I can't stand this boy. He always makes me give in to him. "Hello," I answered as if I was sleepy. "It's me Darius," he shouted. "What's up," I said uninterested. "Baby, how come you haven't called me today?" Before I could answer him, I was disturbed by my thoughts. I know this nigga didn't just ask me that. "Today, I've been tired and sleepy Darius." "So you were sleep all day he asked?" "Yeah," I said sarcastically with a nonchalant tone of voice. "Tiff, I've been trying to call you all day." The phone was silent. "What are you doing Saturday," he slowly asked. "I don't know," I said soft but quickly. "Then tell your mother you have some where to go. My grandfather died and his funeral is Saturday morning." "Are you talking about the man we visited in the hospital a few months ago?" "Yeah," he responded with a low tone of voice. "Look baby, I got some things I need to tell you, but I just don't know how to start. So come straight home after school tomorrow. I'm leaving a letter in the grill on your back porch." The phone was then quiet for three minutes. Darius finally said he'll call me back and we both hung up.

I went on with my night and got up bright and early the next morning. "Hey mom! Good morning." "Good morning girl. Hurry up and eat those cold pancakes I made. I told your butt to get out the bathroom thirty minutes ago Tiffany." "Ma, I need a perm," I said while stuffing my mouth with pancakes. "That's your fault. I told you to take those braids out over the summer time," she said as she walked pass me and flip my kinky pony tail. "Ma, I think I missed my bus this morning, I yelled from the kitchen. Let me drive the car to school since you're off work." "I guess you're still sleep cuz you dam sure ain't stupid. So I'm ma pretend like I didn't hear that," she yelled back. "Ha ha ha ha, La La La La," my little sister sung around me, running from one end of the table to the other in circles.

I left the house in a rush and rode the Marta bus to school. Today was just another ordinary day of classes. I aced a science test and found out the day Te-Te was having her baby shower. As soon as I made it home, I looked on my back porch to see if Darius left a letter in my grill like he said he would. Once again his word was broken because nothing was there. *Bullshit,* is what I said out loud to myself then went back inside. His grandfather probably didn't even die. It was probably an excuse for why he didn't call me that day. I hate to say something like that but the boy is a compulsive liar. I waited all day on his phone call. I tried to give him time but the entire day passed by and when I finally called him, he wasn't home. I don't know what to think when it comes to this boy.

Around eight, I decided to call my best friend, Sundae. I told her to scoop me up so we can go downtown and hang out for a while. We made it downtown around nine o'clock. So hot, everyone was out and hyped up for the weekend. After all it was a Friday night. As Sundae and I got out the car, some guy with his friend came over trying to holla at Sundae. Sundae tells me she hates when most guys come up to her because she has a big butt and that's their main objective. "Excuse me, can I talk to you sexy?" the handsome guy asked Sundae. I looked over to my left and saw two guys probably between the ages of nineteen and twenty-two. The guy talking to Sundae was an attractive, dark skin, tall, athletic built guy. He had gold's in his mouth, which I hate. The other guy was handsome and light skin with a low cut. Sundae looked over her shoulder and responded with the cutest tone of voice. "Naw, shorty, you straight, I have a boyfriend anyway." The guy didn't listen and move in closer on her. Well my name is Jay and this is my partner Greg. Sundae and I continued to ignore them because they were random, but they begin walking with us down the street for whatever reason. I decided to get on my cell phone and Sundae put on headphones as we walked down the street. Neither one of the guys were getting any play so they figured they'd walk us to the corner of the street then leave.

The four of us walked further down the side walk as a crowd around us got thicker and thicker. I told Kayla I'd call her back and asked Sundae what was going on. "Girl I don't know," she said curiously looking over a tall white boy blocking the view. When we reach the other side of the sidewalk I was shock to see what was going on. Through the crowd I could see this dark skin guy between the age of twenty three and twenty six years of age next to a much younger looking girl. He was beating her up as if the police didn't exist or he couldn't be put in jail. The girl looked no older than sixteen in the face but her body was built for the age of an older woman. From looking at the expression on her face she looked as if she's been through the same situation several times before. Even worst, there were a few guys standing there just laughing. I even heard one guy ask the women beater if he can run the train on her later. It was weird watching this as we slowly walked pass because the girl was dead gorgeous and I couldn't understand why her self-esteem was so low. I guess sundae and I were freaked out without realizing it because we both had Jay and Greg close to us as we walked passed. We ended up on the other side of the street talking about the situation and Sundae finally decided to invite them to eat with us.

We went to the underground and ordered some Philly cheese steak sandwiches with fries. The music was blasting with the latest hits and everyone was sporting their latest gear, including me and Sundae. Girls had their hair and nails done as usual and guys were (playing the game) out trying to get as many numbers as possible. After a little side talk, Jay and Greg seemed to be some okay after all. I was in line getting my food when I saw a girl in front of me looking a hot mess. The girl had on super short blue jean shorts that showed her unattractive booty cheeks hanging and a see through tank top. Her friend looked even worst. She had on a pink tank top that said lick me, coochie cutter black shorts, leopard print heels, and long honey blonde weave that fell to the middle of her back. From looking at everyone around me there's no wonder why some females are undesirably treated the way they are from guys. Just like my pastor says, Guys think in their head, *if she is willing to show it then she will probably share it.* Those dimpled butt cheeks put my stomach in a knot as I walked back to the table. An hour later, we were chilling and having a great time talking. Sundae swallowed another fry and looked at Greg with a mean streak. "Me and Jay doing all the talking Greg, so why are you and Tiff so quiet?"

"Man, I'm chilling, he replied. I'm just listening and trying to get know ya'll that's all." While Greg was talking I notice he had a tattoo on his left arm that initialed G.D. At that moment I knew he belonged to a gang. The meaning of G.D. is *The Black Gangster Disciple*, which is a gang that was originally created on the south side of Chicago back in the late 1960's. I decided to ask him about it anyway after I put my drink down. "So what gang are you in Greg?" "What you mean what gang I'm in?" "Well, you got G.D. across your arm, I responded. "Awe, shawdy, that's just some shit I been in since I was eight years old. I didn't really have much of a choice about it at that age and time." "So, umm, are you and Jay coming to Tiffany's birthday party?" Sundae interrupted. "When yo party sexy?" Jay asked as if I was the one asking him. "It's in two weeks at the "Atlanta Skate Pool House" said Sundae quickly. "Well I ain't got nothing to do but make my money. So I'll be there," Greg said with a flirtatious smile.

I leaned in closer to Greg while Sundae and Jay had their own personal conversation. "Just how dooooo you make your money," I asked as I flipped the gold chain Greg wore across his neck. "What you asking me shawdy, if I push weight?" "Yeah that's what I'm asking but I don't think you have to answer that. My question is already answered through the tattoos across your arm." He then tried to pull a fast one on me. "So what's good with you ma, you got a man?" "Yeah I do." "Well can we stay friends or something so I can get to know you?" "What kind of friends?" I asked. "I mean whenever we hook up we can just chill. We can go out to eat or see a movie or something." "I'll think about it," I said.

I thought to myself if he ask me for my number then he's gaming. He suddenly disturbed that very thought by asking me for my phone number. At the same time he put a smile on my face because I found him interesting with distinct character. He's no one I would get serious with but it would be nice to take my mind off Darius. I stopped daydreaming in my thoughts to get rid of the awkward silence between us and spoke in clear words. "Do you have a pen?" He gave me a red pen and I wrote my phone number traditionally in the palm of his hand. Getting late, Sundae and I then left the table to head back to the car.

"OOooOooHHH, this my song girl, Sundae said as she turned the radio up louder. The radio was playing *"I'm still in love with you" by Al Green.* We never did talk about what I had on my mind that night. It was the entire purpose of coming out but I didn't feel like bringing up Darius anyway. I thought I'd just enjoy the ride home and tell her tomorrow. My eyes were closed on the ride home until my phone began vibrating with a bright blue light flashing on and off. The caller I.D. said it was Kayla calling me back so I answered it. "Yeah, it's me what's up Kayla?" "Tiff, what you doing?" "Nothing nigga, what you want at eleven o'clock at night?" "Oh girl, Te-Te is on three-way," she said with excitement. "Girl my water broke, Te blurted out from nowhere. "For real?!!!" I asked eagerly. "Yeah girl, it broke when I was in the car earlier waiting on Kayla to come out the gas station." "Where ya'll at Kayla? We're at DeKalb Medical Hospital." "What room number?" "Room 396 and if they move Te-Te to another room you can just call me on my phone Tiff." "Alright, I'll be there tomorrow morning. Bye niggas," I said as I hung up the phone.

"Who was that?" Sundae asked because I turned down her radio as if my phone call was important. "Girl, it was Te-Te and she's about to have her baby." "Who is Te-Te?" "Nigga you know Te-Te." "Oh, are you talking the girl whose baby daddy got her and another girl pregnant at the same time?" "What? Where you hear that from?" I asked. "I didn't hear it from anywhere," she answered. "I was on the bus going to school the other day and I ran into Carlos. That's his name right?" "Yeah," I said interested in what she was saying. "Well anyway, I didn't even know who he was until he sat by me and told me he sees me in school all the time hanging out with you. After a couple of minutes I figured he was the one who was talking to Tiara but I didn't mention her name in the conversation. So anyway, he kept talking about girls he see me hanging out with and the mutual friends we have in common at school. Then when he said Felisha's name I asked him how he knew her and he said that's my baby momma. I told him I seen Felisha around school last week and she didn't look pregnant to me. He said she's only six weeks pregnant. To make a long story short, the girl Felisha coincidently got on the bus with her sister and they decided to sit directly behind me and Carlos. I guess she got jealous or something because she kept making comments to her sister about me as if I couldn't hear her ass." "Well anyway, keep that to your-self Sundae because I don't know what Te-Te would do if she ever found out. Let me be the one to tell her on my own time." We pulled up to my house and surprisingly all the lights were out. I'm guessing my mother is still at work or something. I got out the car and told Sundae I'll see her later. I wanted to hurry inside before my mom pulled up and catch me standing outside the house. I waved goodbye to Sundae as she drove off and ran upstairs. Oddly, I could feel someone watching me. Nervously, I fumbled with my keys to unlock the door as I suddenly felt a hand stretch from behind me to cover my mouth. In fear, I bit the hand as hard as I could until I saw blood. They let me go. I turned around as quick as possible to see a familiar looking face. "Darius," I shouted out of breath and frighten to death. "Girl you got my hand bleeding," he said as he moved it away from his white ADIDAS shirt. "Boy!!! Come in the house!!! I'm sorry, but you scared me." He sat on the couch while I ran in the bathroom to get some peroxide and a few bandages. I fix the bite on his hand and made him go outside. I didn't want to be caught with him in the house. We sat on the steps and he looked at me as if he had something to say. "Why are you here after 11:30 p.m. Darius?" "Well, you know I went to my great grandfather's funeral. I just had to see you because I got a lot on my mind. Baby life is short. After I came from the funeral, I went to my home boy house. Everything was cool until his mom made him mad. He started cursing at her and I was trying to tell him to calm down cause that's the person he gone need when it all goes down. I even went home and apologize to my mom for when I use to act like that. I know I took a huge risk coming over this late but I been doing a lot of thinking baby. I was thinking we should get married." "My mother would kick me out the house if she knew I was still dating you. So what makes you think we can get married?" "Tiff, I want to marry you regardless of what everyone else is saying. People are going to talk regardless of what we do and even after we are dead. So why worry about the people who are not in this relationship? I mean I know I did my dirt in the past but I'm tired of trying to prove to everybody that I changed. I learned from my mistakes Tiffany!!! I mean, nobody is perfect. The life style I was living was only because I grew up around that and that was all I knew. I grew up around people stealing cars, rims, money, breaking in houses, and taking whatever they wanted in order to live the life they wanted. That's what me and my homeboys did, but I don't do that stuff anymore. I'm not using the way I grew up as an excuse. I now, know the truth. They know nothing about me. You hear me, nothing." Darius continued to talk. "I mean I know people say when you're young that you know nothing about love but I know where I'm coming from. I love you Tiffany and I never felt this way about anyone before. I'm sure when I say I really want to be with you, I mean it. You said, the other day, if your mom finds out about us she's going to send you back to New York, right?" He then stood up and reached out for my hand. Then baby, let's get married so we can be together forever." "Darius I care about you but" . . . . "But what?" he interrupted. "Don't you think we are too young?" I asked him. I mean I have a year of school left and you just finished school not too long ago." He cut me off. "Baby you tell me the day love was born or died. Tell me what love's age is. Love is for anybody who experiences it." "You know what Darius, your grandfather just died. "So I'm ma keep it real with you. I really think you're just talking. You just got some heavy stuff on your mind. Getting married is not going to solve your issues Darius. Look it's late I will see you later." I gave him a hug and watched him slowly walk to his car. He quickly drove off. I went inside to wash my hands clean of peroxide then walked towards my room. As I'm closing my bedroom door I can hear my mother entering the house at the same time. In my street clothes, I quickly hopped in bed. In a panic, I quickly pulled the covers over my dirty clothes and over my head. She opened my door as usual and stood there momentarily making sure everything was okay. I closed my eyes tight, barely moving an inch. I thought to myself, if only two more minutes would have passed by while Darius was here, all of hell would have broke loose. My heart finally stopped pounding hard as she closed my bedroom door.

Chapter Three

Push baby, push one more time Tiara said Ms. Jackson. "I can't do this ma," Te-Te screamed out loud. "Yes you can," her mother said with a supportive tone of voice. "Come on girl one more hard push." Kayla and I stood on the side of the bed trying not to look. All right, we can see the head, said the doctor. Everybody in the room was excited except Carlos who was busy throwing up in a purple cup the doctor gave him earlier. It took six minutes for the baby to come out completely. She came out screaming and hollering as if her mother took too long to push her out. AAUUGGGHHH!!!!! Kayla and I said at the same. The baby was full of Te-Te's blood. Oddly, the baby was covered with purple and white body fluids. I guess it was okay because the doctor said she was healthy. The baby turned out to be fourteen inches long and weighed seven pounds. Kayla and I decided to stay with Te-Te the rest of the night. The next morning Te-Te woke up screaming about pain in her stomach. The nurse told her to relax and gave her some pain medicine. Kayla and I didn't get any sleep from the hard chairs in the hospital so we left early.

The day after, I was sitting in my business class, browsing the computer, until my girl China came in with a really bad attitude. She came over to sit in her assigned seat but a freshman was sitting at her computer. She walked up behind him and slapped him silly up-side his head like an annoying little brother. "Fool, get out of my seat. You already know. I don't know why you sat here in the first place," she said with rage and anger. He quickly turned around making sure no one saw a girl hit him across the head. "A girl, I don't know what's your problem but you need to calm down." "Get up then," she said as she hit him again. "You know what? I'll hate to do something that I'll regret because of anger. So I'm ma get up now." "Stuck up trick," he mumbled under his breath as he walked passed me. "I heard that boy, I shouted in my friend's defense."

Something must really be wrong with China, I thought to myself because she's never this angry. China sat by me the entire class period looking stubborn. She finally turned towards me with tears in her eyes. She moved a little closer and lowered her voice so others around us couldn't hear her. "Tiff, I need somebody to talk to." "What's wrong China?" I asked concerned. "My boyfriend is cheating on me." "What happened and how do you know that?" "Girl I just know. I can just tell by the way he's been acting lately. He called me on my lunch break to ask me if he could pick this girl up because she needs a ride to the church. I know the girl and I know she go to our church by why in the hell does my man have to give her a ride. I mean her house is out of the way, anyway.

It just doesn't make since to me. She trying to act like she's a member of the church and a good friend of me and my man's, but I know she wants him. He playing stupid like he don't know what's going on and all she want is a ride. I'm just tired of playing games Tiffany. What would you do Tiff?" "Honestly, girl you asking the wrong person," I said laughing. "But serious China, I would just tell him how I feel. Also, I would tell her the only time she need to be getting a ride is when I'm around. If the girl has any respect for you and she's the innocent church member like she's trying to be, then she won't have a problem with respecting what you told her." "Tiff, I need your new number." I stood up to give her my new cell number. Here China here is a poem I wrote called "Free Again" a long time ago. I want you to read it out loud and be positive. "Okay, wait Tiff. I wanna read it now. China unfolded the pink piece of paper.

Free Again

Thank God
I used him to build
Instead of
Break me
Walking away a stronger
Woman internally
My urge is stronger to find
True destiny
Time is a blessing
To explore the inner
Parts of me
Back on the ***journey***
To conquer
What belongs to ***me***
Bringing out great ***abilities***
To change and create
My ***reality***
No longer ***existing***

But ***living***
Freedom is a ***blessing***
My strength overcomes and
Keep me moving

After she read it, we embrace one another and left the class twenty minutes after everyone else.

As soon as I got home, I took off my boots and shook the dead leaves off the bottom. I fix myself some hot chocolate and took a long hot bath to relax my muscles. Man, I got to get in the gym and work out. Just because you look good on the outside does not mean you're in shape. I was on the phone with Sundae about some homework until suddenly my father called me on the other line.

I click over. "Hello," I answered. "This is your father," the voice on the other end of the phone responded. "Hello dad, how is everything going?" "Everything is fine but your grandma not doing so well. I'm steady sending her back and forth from the hospital. Listen, I was calling to let you know when you come to Detroit your coming to stay with me." "My mother told me I could stay with my uncle." "I don't care what your mother said.

I'm your father and what I say goes. Remember, that I'm your father and you're not none of mines." Then my father begins talking about a load of stuff I could care less of hearing. I have never met a man to hire lawyers to fight what he owes in child support. I basically kept quiet so he could run out of stuff to say. "Yeah okay dad," I said to rush him off the phone. I click back over to Sundae and didn't say a single word. "What's wrong with you? Was that Darius, Tiff?" "No," I said with a bad attitude. "What's your problem then?" "Man my dad is getting on my nerves." "You know what Tiffany, I'm tired of hearing about your dad and you not telling me anything about it.

So either you tell me the truth of why you don't get along with your father or stop talking about it," she said in a demanding tone of voice. "It's just a lot of stuff that's been built up over the years Sundae." "Okay girl I'm listening." "I mean, to be honest with you, I love my father but I don't like him Sundae. He doesn't deserve respect. I mean, Sundae he doesn't treat me like he use to because I'm older but I remember days I didn't feel good about myself because of him.

I guess that's why I became closer to God at an early age because God was my FATHER, both physically and spiritually. When I was a young girl Sundae, my father didn't do the things you would think a father was supposed to do. He was just verbally abusive, demanding, and controlling.

To make a long story short Sundae he wasn't there for me then and he's not here for me now. Hold on Sundae my line is beeping." "Hello," I answered kind of shaky. "What's wrong?" the other voice asked. "Mom," I cried out. "Why don't you just give him his money back?" "Tiff, I don't know why you let him get to you like this. What did he say to you?" "Ma, hold on. I need to hang up with Sundae." "Hurry up Tiff. I'm at work." I quickly clicked back over to Sundae then hung up. "Ma, He basically was talking about me coming to Detroit. And how he's going to fight the child support case because he doesn't feel as if he owes the amount he was sentence to. I'm upset because all he talks about is money.

What nerve of him to think it's okay and normal to have a conversation with me about him not paying child support? Sounds like a man who is still not taking full responsibility." "Well Tiffany like I told you before, don't feel bad because that is money he owe me for the several times I paid for everything on my own. He got a lot nerves.

Do you think if I sign those papers over telling the court that he can keep the money that he will send you a single red dime? Look, I'm at work. So we'll have to finish talking about this when I get home. This is stressing me out and I'm not about to let this stress me out Tiffany. Girl, I can remember when you were about twelve and you use to write all kind of hateful poems about him because he wasn't there. Do you remember that?" "Yeah, I do. Mom, I will just talk to you when you get home later." When I got off the phone with my mother, I broke down in tears. My four year old brother didn't know what to do so he cried with me telling me don't cry.

For some reason, my father always touched the pain of my heart without even knowing how bad it hurts. Even though I have a father, my life is still absent from having a real father. In my eyes, the child support money was and still is more important to my father to not pay it then making an effort to spend time with me. When it comes to money I've always been second in his life. My heart is an effort my father never tried to find within himself to accomplish. For example, it's been over seven years since we moved down south and not one time has he come to visit. The last conversation with him was about him having another grown child. It's a boy and he supposed to be in college. My father is just a person who can't ever admit to being wrong about anything. I studied my homework the rest of the night and went to sleep. The next morning seniors at Rosewood High School had a senior meeting at two o'clock. My friends and I, including the entire committee, gave our senior leader a standing ovation.

This was our fifth senior meeting and we only been in school for two months now. This was our homecoming week for Rosewood. "Hello fellow students, as you all know I'm Tracy Dawson. I've talked it over with Mr. Brown to let us have our senior trip in Mexico but ladies and gentlemen you have to pay your senior dues. I can't emphasize that enough. Seniors, we are role models this year, she said with excitement. The under classmen are watching our every move, so behave.

Also, I want to see everyone at graduation. So let's cut down on skipping class, she said jokingly. I'm so excited this school year and I hope this senior year give us all memories we will never forget. Okay, I have a couple of announcements I need to make about the following weeks. First, the next senior meeting will be held in the cafeteria next Thursday at two-thirty.

Also, it's time to take pictures for our school yearbook. Pictures will take place in three days which is Wednesday at one o'clock. At last, we're having senior skate night at *Rainbow Rinker's* on the sixteenth of this month. Thank you, senior class. We're going to have great year."

Chapter Four

What up, what up, what up Rosewood? Is the music in here hot or what? Come on ladies, I don't want to see nobody on the wall. If you don't want to be here then go home to your mama. Everyone including myself laughed at the D J as he continued. "I want to see some food. I want to see some skating. I definitely want to see some ladies dancing with some fellows up in here tonight. Let's drop it like its hot people." The DJ then put on a record and begin talking to different people for more song request. I'm really enjoying myself because tonight is Rosewoods high school skate party and my girls and I are chilling at the table with other seniors from school. The party is *crunk*. Everyone is wearing red and white to represent our school colors and the place is pack from wall to wall. Rosewood is not a big high school so it's obvious that other high school students are here as well supporting our school. "Girl, look at that fine boy rocking that black to your left, Sundae said with a smile." "Sundae, I hope *looooooookkkking* is all you plan on doing because that's Ericka's man, Kayla said." "Will ya'll chill. Ya'll act like he's the only guy in here," I blurted in a joking tone voice They both told me to shut up at the same time and laughed. "I'll be back. I need to get something to drink," I said getting up from the table. "Bring me back a juice," Kayla hollered. I skated over to the concession stand and couldn't believe who I saw tongue kissing another girl. It was Carlos, Te-Te's boyfriend. I was wondering if Sundae's accusations in the car were true. I didn't want him to see me but I did want to find out what was going on. So I skated to the left of the blue lockers where they couldn't see me. Then I moved a little closer so I could hear over the loud music. I heard the Felicia girl giggling. "So like I was saying sexy, you gone let me come over tonight or what?" Carlos asked in a deep playa tone of voice. "I don't know she said softly. Te-Te? Whatever happened to that girl people say you had a baby with Carlos?" "Oh yeah, but I mean that's just my baby momma. We don't talk like that anymore and I only go around her to see the baby, that's it." I was listening to them and glancing at the same time. The girl Carlos was with had on some small Baby Phat red shorts and a white polo shirt short enough to show her green butterfly belly ring. Carlos cell phone began ringing but he ignored it. Finally he answered it quickly then hung up. "Look sexy, I got to take care of some business but don't forget what we talked about." As the girl walk away he slapped her on her butt as if he's been there and done that. He pressed a number on speed dial and began arguing with someone. "Girl I told you I was at the school skate party, Carlos shouted with a nasty attitude. Why you keep sweating me Te. I'm tired of dealing with you, he claimed." He then grew silent and I could only imagine all the screaming he was hearing from the other end of the phone. "Look here girl, I'll call you back when you calm down." Carlos then hung up the phone like he was the man.

I moved over and switched positions as he began walking over to the D J table with a huge smile as if nothing ever happened. I hurried up and got the food I needed from the concession stand then headed back to the table with Sundae and Kayla. "What took you so long girl?" Kayla asked but really didn't want to know. "Shut up, the line was long," I responded like a big sister. After ten minutes my girls left me at the table alone and went to the dance floor. I didn't feel like dancing so I figured I'd go to the outdoor swimming pool and relax for a while.

The pool was beautiful. It was shaped like a huge spiral circle with colorful yellow and green lights in the water. The music was different from the dance floor but everyone seems to be enjoying it. From what I observed, it was a very relaxing environment where couples were enjoying themselves and having a great time eating and talking to one another. Everyone was wearing the glow in the dark red wrist bands the skating rink gave to Rosewood students. There were a few seniors floating on different color floats in the pool goofing off. I love how the employees of this facility decorated the trees with red and white lights to support our school event. I wore my swimsuit under my clothes and caught a few eyes watching me as I transitioned. I then sat on the edge of the pool and dipped my pink pedicured toes in the warm water. I began thinking about Darius because once again he went M.I.A. I then felt a soft hand on my shoulder.

Without looking, my instincts told me it must be a girl. I turned around and saw China. "China!! Hey girl, what's up?" I got up to give her a huge hug and she had the biggest smile I ever seen on her face. "Tiffany, I want to you meet Derrick." "Hey, what's up Derrick," I said as I held out my hand to shake his. "That's what I'm trying to find out because the party in here is hot tonight," he said as he gave me dap like I was one of his home boys. "We just came from dancing girl, China said. I made Derrick come out here because I'm ready to relax Tiff. I saw Kayla on the dance floor and she told me I would probably find you out here. I just wanted to see you girl but we about to grab something to eat. So I'll see you later Tiff." "Okay," I said. As China and Derrick walked away, China looked back at me waiting for my approval of Derrick.

I gave her two thumbs up. In my opinion, Derrick carried himself like a well-mannered down to earth guy. The boy had his pants on his ass and sound educated so that's a great start in my book. Plus he's a member of her church, the president of a youth group, and get straight A's in school. "That's good China," I said out loud to myself. I looked down by my side and saw an envelope with my name on it saying it was from china. When she put this here, I said out loud to myself. I open the letter and it was a poem she wrote. China always was a good writer so I read it out loud.

It was called "Understand Me"

"Understand Me"

I have to love myself under all
Circumstances, conditions,
and situations,
Unconditionally,
and **eternally.**
I have be sure of me
confidently
It's the only sure way to
love you
genuinely
I can only love you

To the height of my
Compatible
Ability But . . . .
To conquer my heart
You must go through the
Father **Spiritually**
There I wait for you
Anxiously

I thought the poem was sweet and short. I'm assuming it's how she feels about the new guy she's dating. I put the poem neatly back in its envelope.

"What is good?" a familiar voice asked from behind me. I turn to my right and surprisingly see Greg standing there. "Boy, what you doing here?" I asked playfully. He gave me a friendly hug then sat down to dip his feet in the pool. "Sundae invited me when we were at the underground eating, remember?" "Yeah, but I didn't expect you to come. She was just making conversation." He paused. "So this is your skate party huh?" "Yeah," I said as we both laughed. "Okay I'm caught," I said.

"It's not really my skate party as you can already see. It's actually my high school that's throwing the skate/pool party. "Now that I've thought about it, I didn't even tell you the address Greg. How did you find out where to find the party?" Well, your girl kind of put me up on game in a phone call conversation a few days later and told me you wanted me to come." "I just smiled at him embarrassingly, knowing Sundae probably made me sound desperate when she called Greg."

The entire night, we played around in the pool and had a great time. We enjoyed each other's conversation. I tried to not like him no more than a friend, but it failed. Greg was light skin with a wavy low cut and warm brown eyes that could make you melt. It's ironic, I find him attractive because light skin guys are not my type.

I guess each individual is simply an individual, not a color. Sundae told me a few days ago that he really liked me and asked her a hundred and one questions about me and Darius. It was finally the last hour of the night so Greg and I dried off. We went to the dance floor to grab Sundae and Jay but ended up dancing the last hour with them instead. "Can ya'll give us a ride home?" I asked screaming over the music. "Yeah shawdy. Ya'll can ride with us," said Greg. They dropped us off at Sundae's house an hour later around 11:30pm.

Chapter Five

That's right!!! Amen, the lady on the side of me kept screaming like she was filled with the Holy Spirit. There were only a few minutes of church left and our Pastor was calling people to the front who wanted to make Jesus Christ their personal savior and rededicate their life to God. "The devil is a loser and he's about to lose you," Pastor said with a sincere voice. "You have to be saved before it's too late and I'm telling you beloved, we are living in our last days. So if you are in your seat and your heart is crying to Jesus then come on down and don't hesitate." I gathered my things and walked down the aisle. My heart was beating so fast but I knew I was doing the right thing regardless of who was watching me or what people thought of me. My pastor looked stunned when he saw my face. "How are you doing, Tiffany?" "I'm fine Pastor Johnson." "Okay, well, walk to the prayer room with one of the deacons to assist you." I walked to the back and prayed with my prayer partner. I've had the same prayer partner since I was twelve years old. I told her the sins I committed with my ex boyfriend and I wanted to turn my life back over to God.

She asked me why I didn't pray to God the first and second time I sinned. I told her I felt ashamed and dirty before God and didn't feel worthy. She took my hand and told me to never feel that way again. She told me that God want me to come to him as I am. She told me to never stay away from God because the devil wants me to feel unworthy after sinning. She said to always repent and come back to God because God loves me unconditionally. She said there is no sin that is not already forgiven and erased by God.

I walked out of church guiltless, with courage. Now the biggest challenge will be living the way I'm supposed to live but I'm ready to fight for the person I really am. The next morning I walked to my favorite park called Piedmont Park located in Midtown of Atlanta. It was a chilly day. So I grabbed some hot chocolate on the way. I sat on my favorite bench and read this drama book about a girl who got pregnant at the age of thirteen. Of course I began writing. I put my pen and paper down and took a long look from the swing bench I sat on.

"Man I love this park," I said out loud to myself. There are people riding their bikes, jogging, walking their dogs, playing catch, picnicking on the grass, roller skating, feeding the ducks, and so many other things. It feels good to get away and just be alone in peace. I got up from the bench and went to my favorite ice cream parlor on the corner of North Avenue. There's a lot of traffic for some reason today. To my left a lady was screaming out her car window because a man jumped in front of the car without looking. That's some serious road rage I thought to myself. I walked through the traffic and entered the store. "Hey sweetie," said a familiar lady with a deep southern. Let me guess "two huge scoops of vanilla ice cream with chocolate fudge, almond nuts, and caramel sauce, right?" "Yes ma'am," I said with a polite smile. After I got my ice cream, I took the long way home on the train. I sat down and put my head phones up to my ear so I could write more poetry. Everyone on the train just looked so tired and beat up from working a job. Fifteen minutes later, my phone rung with Anthony's name on the screen. "Hey Tiff, how you doing?" "I'm good," I said. I knew in my head something had to be wrong because

Anthony only call me when he is desperately trying to get in contact with Darius. "When was the last time you talk to Darius?" "Friday, why Anthony?" "Well, what's going on with him Tiff?" "What do you mean?" I asked. "I mean is he still going to school and working or did he drop out again?" My mouth fell opened wide. I didn't even know the boy dropped out of school the first time, I thought to myself. The shock I felt paralyzed my mouth for a few seconds.

"Hello, Tiff?"

"Yeah, I'm here" I said. "What's wrong? You didn't know or something?" "No Anthony, he never even told me. Since we go to different high schools, I guess he decided to keep it from me," I sadly said. "Look Tiffany, I honestly think you're too smart and pretty for Darius. If you ever want to know something just let me know and I'll tell you." "Okay, so is this your number Anthony?" "Naw, this is a temporary number but my main number is (404) 555-1110." I wrote Anthony's number down and hung up the phone.

I got off the train and called Sundae for a ride home from the station near my house. I told her about the conversation I had with Anthony before she dropped me off.

Monday, I went to school depress. I came home and my mother went to work as usual. My mind no longer belonged to me. I wanted to find out everything about Darius because I didn't know him. This boy's entire life is a lie. Shit, I'm starting to wonder what the hell his real name is. I called Anthony later on that night because I've never felt so alone and lost in a relationship. I felt like I've ruined my relationship with God because of sin and hid from my mother just to realize my entire relationship was and still is a lie. I just don't get this shit. Darius is so sweet and nice to me but then he will go M.I.A. I've tried my best to believe the boy isn't cheating and think positive about him but this is some straight up, wide open, bullshit.

I picked up the phone to call Anthony with all of these questions in my head. "Hello?" "Hey Ant, it's Tiff!" "Oh hey Tiffany, what's up?" "I need to ask you something." "What?" "What else is there I need to know about Darius?" "Look Tiff, I'll put it to you like this, whatever you ask I'll tell." "Has he ever cheated on me?" "Yeah, I think so." "When?" I asked. "I'd say this summer, Anthony said. "How do you know and with who?" I asked. "This summer we went over this girl name Trish house. As a matter of fact I know for a fact he hit that because when we went over there she didn't have on anything but a t-shirt." "What else I need to know." "Well remember when he had that Black Planet Page some time ago?" "Yeah", I responded with pain and anger. "He use to talk to girls on there and every time we went somewhere he'll drop me off at home and be like I gotta catch up with later nigga. I got to go over this and that girl house." "Anthony, I said calmly, exactly when was he having sex with Trish?" "It was this summer like early June."

"Also, those boys he be with, got him smoking weed. It seems like every nigga he hang with be getting him in trouble. Darius is just messing up everybody's life Tiff. Everybody he meets he screws it up. Darius act different around you Tiff but don't let that nigga fool you because I've known him for a much longer time. I use to do some of the same garbage he does. Tiffany, you can do better. By the way Tiff, he's Darius around you, but on the street, that nigga name is Jo-Jo and that's all I'm going say about that." "Yeah, well, at this point it doesn't matter because it's over between us," I said with tears in my eyes. I then hung up the phone and slammed it on the kitchen table. Something inside of me never did trust him and now that I know the truth I would think I'd be crying on my kitchen floor but instead I feel totally different. I feel free and happier than I've been in the past year. All the energy and negative gut feelings I had worrying about where he is and who he is with is finally over. Something inside of me was turn't up.

I turned on a gospel c d and began dancing like a free run-away slave. I began thanking God for revealing the truth and started praising him like never before. The burden of worrying about my mother finding out, having a lost soul, worrying about Darius cheating, and losing God's favor was finally over. Now all I have to do is wait for my ex to call and tell him to his sorry face.

Up late doing homework, the phone rang. I hopped up knowing it was Darius calling me. Hello, I answered. "Hey baby what's up?" "Nothing," I said with a bad attitude. "Baby if you mad about Friday, I'm sorry. I know I was supposed to come over but I was out with some friends and lost track of time." "It's a lot deeper than Friday Darius. Look, I'm ma make this simple and easy for the both of us. It's over Darius!!! I don't ever want to see you again." I then hung up the phone. He called me back and of course I answered it. "What Darius?" "What the hell is wrong with you?" "Don't act stupid with me boy. You know you been doing dirt behind my back." "Baby what's up?" "I'm not your baby my name is Tiffany." "What have you been doing all summer Darius? Better yet who you been doing?

You know what Darius, don't even answer those questions. As far as I'm concern you can continue to sleep with whom the hell ever because it's over between us." "Tiffany, who are you talking about?" "Who is Trish?" I asked. "I don't even know a Trish. What are you talking about Tiff?" "Oh you can't think back to June of this year. "I'm telling you I don't know a girl name Trish. I wasn't doing nothing but working in June. Tiff, baby you think I would do that to you? Who's been telling you this stuff?" "Does it matter?" I asked in a very angry tone. "Yes, it does matter," he said. "Anthony told me." "Look Tiff, I'm not about to argue with you." "I hate you Darius." "Tiffany, stop this before I come over there." "I don't care if you come over here because I'll never let you in my house again." Tiff, whatever it is, I didn't do it." "You know what Darius, it's hard to believe any words coming from your mouth right now. Why would Anthony tell me you did then if you didn't?" "Look Tiff, Anthony is just mad about his money. I mean, I love him like a brother but we going through some stuff that's a whole lot deeper than money right now. I'm not about to start on me and Anthony but just listen to me Tiff. How can you just believe him without even asking me at least?" "Darius I don't want to hear that because if Sundae told you something like that about me you'll believe her too." "I mean, yeah, I would because I know Sundae be around you all the time but I would still come to you and at least ask you about it." "Tiff, I'm telling you the truth whether you like it or not. I didn't do it and I would never do that to you. Man, my arm is all mess up. I was in a car accident early this morning.

I came home to call you for comfort and you give me this garbage about Anthony. Anthony is just mad about his money and will do and say whatever it takes to ruin me right about now. You know what Tiff I was going to wait to tell you this because

I didn't know how to tell you this but I'm leaving to go to the army in three weeks. I'm leaving for South Carolina on the 30th of next month.

I love you, Tiffany. Since day one, I've treated you with the up most respect." "Darius promise me you're not lying." "I promise you Tiffany." "I have to go, I said confused and back in the same spot I've been in for months. "Darius, do you honestly care about this relationship?" "Yes, of course Tiffany." "Can I, Can I, Can I call you tomorrow?" "NO . . . . because I don't trust you." I then hung up in his face. After I hung up the phone I felt as if I was trapped again. I was emotionally, verbally, spiritually, and physically stressed. I was tired and fell asleep on the couch. I went to school the next morning and told Sundae what happened during our lunch hour. She gave me a hug. "Tiffany it's time to move on and now I see what your mother is talking about. Tiffany if you stay with him you'll only keep on giving him chances.

Girl I can count on my hand how many chances you gave that boy." "He said he didn't do it Sundae. I'm just confused because I don't know who is telling the truth. Is Anthony telling me this to get revenge on Darius because he's mad about his money or was Anthony mad about his money and told the truth on Darius?" "Tiff, we are both seventeen and I haven't been through half the stuff you been through girl. Do you know what that means, Tiff?" "What?" I asked. "It means stop letting that fool fill your head up with *bullshit*. As your best friend Tiff, I'm telling you to move on." "Thanks Sundae," I said as I got up and headed towards class. I looked at her from a far and said out loud to myself, I'm just confused on what I feel and what's really real. I then walked out the cafeteria and went to my last class.

The day went on quickly and I dragged home after school. I started on my homework and had the phone sitting next to me hoping Darius was telling the truth. At 3:29pm he pops up over my house. During the day we act as if nothing ever happened. Later that night the drama came to light. "So are you going to tell me or what?" I asked? Darius looked me dead in my eyes and said Tiffany you know I didn't do it. I left his answer as that and left the conversation alone. It was that moment I knew he was a fucking liar. I figured the boy was leaving in three weeks anyway so I wanted to stick around for the truth to air out because I knew it was a matter of time before the *BULLSHIT SMELLS.* We watched TV and cuddled on the front room couch.

We then went to the room and had a serious conversation about "US", even though everything went in my right ear and out the other. After watching t v for so long it was starting to get late. We started wrestling and playing like we normally do. Then Darius kiss my neck. Then he kissed my stomach and down my back. My hormones were strong but I didn't want to respond to them. "I want to do something different this time," he said out of the blue. He turned over and asked me what I wanted to do. I said nothing. "What do you want to do?" I asked him. Before he could respond, I responded. "Well whatever it is, I want to get straight to the point," I said unsure of his motives. Then in disappointment I found out what he wanted. He climbed on top of me and pushed inside of me. I thought to myself I can't believe he would have sex with me after I told him last week that I was struggling with God. It was the same process we always did and like usual he'll get a thrill out of it but to me it didn't feel good at all. During sex, I rolled my eyes wishing he would hurry up. Then I notice something about him. As we were having sex, I was staring at his face while he was looking down at the sex. It was then, I knew he was screwing me and not loving me. The fact that I don't have a ring from this boy is enough said as far as love goes anyway. "Tiffany, you want to get on top?" "It doesn't matter, I said trying to be nice but dam sure didn't want to do it. He took that answer for a yes because he flipped me over quickly as I found myself on top of him. I was disgusted. I got on top of him and did a moderate speed but he then took his hands and placed them at my hips. He viciously pulled me up and down with all his strength so I went along with the flow. He was starting to hurt me. I wanted him to hurry up and come. I don't know why I'm doing this or why in the hell I'm with this boy I thought to myself. He finally let go and let me control the speed but it was still senseless to me. I can't believe I'm doing this I said again in my head.

I made him leave right after with a lie about needing to do some homework. I felt so used and I cried out to God asking him to forgive me. I felt dirty, ashamed, used, and confused. I sat in the bath tub for over 2 hours quietly crying as I washed my body until it turned red. Unfortunately, I couldn't wash away the low self-esteem I must have had when I slept with him. Deep in my heart I know I only did it to *BE BETTER THAN THE NEXT.* I hated myself for what I did for someone else's pleasure instead of my own. My pleasure is God. Before I went to bed that night I found an old note I wrote in my room.

IT READS:

A "coward" is a person who turns down their true self by doing out of character activities due to fear. A coward does not own up to responsibilities. I closed the note I wrote and took it to heart. I felt like I was destroying my soul. I opened up my diary.

Dear diary, this is how I feel about my situation with Darius right now. I then wrote my emotions down and turned them into a poem. "Love-Trol" was the title.

Love-Trol

Fake love can keep u
From saying what u really want
And from walking away from
What u really **should**
When it's wrong it can feel so **good.**

It can keep you in when you're
Looking for a way **out**
Making you feel so crazy inside
because your mind is far **out**.

It'll keep you smothered
When your grasping for **air**
Keeping your character out of
space because you're not **there.**

When you have doubt
It'll keep you simple minded
Believing only one thing to be **true**
You'll overlook it until
Doubt has control over **you**.

It's something that
Can trap you **inside**
You may stay when it's
wrong because it feel so **right**

Taking control **mentally**
Controlling everything **physically**

whether positively or **abusively**
it's awakened constantly because its
Phenomenally just **lovely**
When it **controls**,
But that reason is because it's not love
Its **love-trol**

Chapter Six

Two weeks has passed by and I'm going through days existing instead of living. I was making a sandwich in the kitchen and ease dropping on my mother's phone conversation at the same time. "You know what honey? I'm just going to leave your aunty alone because you can't tell a woman who is in love nothing. She's not going to leave him even if the truth is in her face. Fake love got a way of covering up the answers you need." Everything around me seems to be giving me clues about my situation. Today was Sunday and we didn't go to church because my mother had to work. "Ma, are you still braiding my hair today?" "Yeah, hurry up before I don't feel like it." Later on that day, I threw on some clothes and played card games at Sundae house for the night. The very next day Darius came to my house to visit. Later on, oddly, he put some money in my purse. Darius will give me time but money was always a non-factor for him. Since we both were jobless and in high school, I didn't think much of it. Sometimes when I think back on how we met, friends should have been the result. He honestly never was compatible on a boyfriend/

girlfriend level. I met Darius while playing a game of truth or dare. My best female friend at the time named Image was crazy about Darius best friend James. The dare was for me to date Darius for two weeks while she dates James for two weeks. I did it because behind closed doors she begged me. I was never attracted to Darius from the beginning but as time went pass I was attracted to the good way he treated me. Then he asked me if we could continue afterwards and I said yes. I gave him a chance because he was a sweet heart. That's the history and beginning of me and Darius. My mother never cared for the boy since the first time she saw him. My mother's words have been bothering me but she is right. A man should show that he cares and if he can't buy you anything on special days like your birthday then, hell, he should have made you something. It's about the effort a person puts into the situation. Anyway, like I was saying, It's Monday and Darius came over to visit. We were watching TV when he decided out the blue to put some money in my unzipped purse. He was counting on the side of my room like he was counting hundred dollar bills slowly and carefully. How about an hour later, I went in my purse while he went to the bathroom and I counted seven dollars in my purse. I didn't want him to know I looked in my purse so I didn't say anything to him about it after he came from the bathroom. Later on we argued about something really stupid (not money) so I left my room and went into the front room to watch t v. Next thing I knew Darius left out my room and slammed the front room door behind him. A bad feeling sat in my stomach about him taking his money back. So I went in my room to see if he took the seven dollars. As soon as I opened my door I could see my unzipped purse was now half zipped. I unzip the other half and the money was gone. This fool was so selfish that he took back his *funky seven dollars like I was going to miss it.* I called my girl Kayla and she bust out in tears laughing after I told her. I guess I'll laugh later down the road but right now I'm piss. I couldn't help but think of what my pastor preached during the past Sunday sermon. He said a boy can tell you he loves you a thousand times but after a while you're going to get tired of hearing it and want him to show it. I don't know how much longer I can take being with this boy. He got two more weeks.

Chapter Seven

I'm ready to die Tiffany, just leave me alone!!! "I don't know what to do. I'm scared. I don't know what it's like to be a teen mom on my own," Te-Te screamed from the top of her lungs. Here I am at my girl Te-Te house trying to get her to come down from standing over the outside of her balcony. She is currently hanging from a rail on the ninth floor. She found out Carlos was cheating on her and had another baby on the way in five months.

When she called me over the phone an hour ago she had a normal sounding voice. I grabbed hot chocolate from my house. I decided to come over to comfort her and have small chat but I had no idea I would find her over a balcony flirting with death. What if I didn't even come over here I thought in my head. In a panic I called Carlos and told him to come as soon as possible. "Please Tiara come down girl. I love you so much. Te-Te, the pain will go away," I said as I tried to move in closer to grab her. The thought of my friend killing herself broke me down. I couldn't hold back my tears. She looked back at me "I gave everything I had because I thought that's what he was giving me," she said pointing to herself. "This fool has a baby on the way and I know my fantasy of being with him forever is over . . . . and so am I" . . . . she said hopelessly as if the world was coming to an end. "Look Tiff,

I hung up with you so I could do this alone. Not so you could rush over here and try to save me." "My mind is made up," she screamed. "I just feel so stupid and worthless. I even proved that I loved him by getting pregnant on purpose. He thinks it was accident but I know I did it on purpose. I'm not good enough anymore Tiffany and don't you dare say I am because I know I did you wrong too." "Let me tell you something Tiara, no one is worth you dying over. Do you understand me Te? Everyone has an issue from time to time but you'll get through it one way or another and as your friend I'll always be one way.

You don't have to stay with Carlos just because you had his baby." "Tiffany, all I can think about is the night he told me he love me." "So what," I screamed at her. "I remember the day I told you that I loved you" I said from the top of my lungs. "Tiffany you just don't understand. "I'm so hurt that I'm taking my own life," she screamed with tears in her eyes. Wow I can't believe I just said that she said. "TIFFANY I'M SO FUCKING HURT THAT I'M TAKING MY OWN LIFE", she screamed out loud again. "Can you imagine pain so great that you want to die? "No," I said with a very low tone of voice. "I feel like my heart is dying from the harsh truth of Carlos." I tried to move closer to Tiara while she was talking. "Tiff, get away from me she," said as a threat. "If you come any closer, I swear, I will jump." I stop in my tracks trying to think of another way to approach her. My last thought was to just go for it. I thought to run and grab her. I rather take a chance on grabbing her than to watch her let go on her own. So I went for it. As soon as I got half way she was hanging on by a pinky finger. The look in her face told me she was already dead. The look in her face told me she was determined to let go before I reached her. And she did . . . . I reached over the rail and caught Tiara by her left foot. My heart is beating fast as I'm struggling to hold her body weight daggling over the rail. Hold on Te, I said straining to keep my feet on the ground. Te-Te then kicked me in my face with her other foot. "Let me go Tiffany. Let me go bitch." The kick caused me to lose my balance.

At this very moment I'm not sure if I should let her go to save my life or continue holding on to her. The only objects I see are the toy cars beneath us. Suddenly, I realized both of my feet are off the ground now and in a matter of seconds I'm about to die with her. As soon as I was about to let her go, I felt more than one pair of hands holding me. I heard several voices behind me yelling and shouting hold on Tiff just hold on. I assumed one of those voices belonged to Carlos. Te-Te and I were pulled back over the balcony with force. Hard breathing was the only thing heard for a while. Te-Te then grabbed me tight and cried like never before. She just kept saying I'm Sorry Tiffany, I'm so sorry. I held her and so did Carlos. Carlos friends waited in the living room. Three weeks later Te-Te went through counseling and made good progress for herself and the baby. I never mentioned that day to her again. Surprisingly, Carlos began going to counseling sessions with her. Te-Te's family said he was only going because of the guilt. Carlos and Te-Te decided they were better off not being together but Carlos promise to be there for the baby. I now realize how special life is and to never take it for granted. I, myself, shouldn't be tied down to anyone at the age of seventeen. I think one of the biggest mistakes teenagers make is falling in love too soon. Your teenage years are simply for dating only. You should date people and not get serious until college at least. During your teenage years you should only be finding out who you are deep inside and what you want to do with the rest of your life beyond high school. You should be chasing your passion, skill, or talent, nothing more. After Te-Te's incident, everything in my life went on as usual. I went to school, hung out with my friends and family, and kept on living. Two more weeks went passed and I went over to Sundae's house in the afternoon. Her aunt walked in the living room coming from work. She threw her bag on the couch as hard as she could and just looked at us. Then she screamed out of what looks like frustration.

"What's wrong?" Sundae asked as she stood up from the floor. "Sundae baby, I was laid off today." "That's not fair," Sundae said. "Yeah baby, well, that's why you don't need a job honey. You need a business of your own Sundae. Listen to what I tell you because times are different now." Ms. Denise took off her heels and told us she'll fix us dinner later. "That's okay," Sundae yelled down the hallway. "We're going out to eat aunty." "Don't come back too late she shouted back before she closed her bedroom door.

"Girl, guess what?" Sundae blurted out. "I don't know, what?" I asked. "I got some tickets to the concert you wanted to go to. "Really?" I asked with enthusiasm. "Yeah girl!" "But it's today," I said. "Duh, I know that Tiff. That's why I made up the lie about going out to eat so we can sneak to the concert. When we get there I'll just call my aunt and tell her I'm staying the night at your house so we can stay out later. Then when she goes to work in the morning we can just come back here." "Well, where you get the tickets dummy?" I asked. "Actually," Sundae said with hesitation. "Actually what?" I asked. "Actually, Greg and Jay invited us and these are the tickets they gave me." "What!!!!" "Tiffany, why you trippen?" "We're just going to chill and have a good time." "Stop thinking about that asshole Darius because the liar is not thinking about you." "Fine," I said as we left the house. "Come on Tiffany, you need to walk faster before we miss the bus," she said as she pushed me from behind. I was wondering earlier why Sundae told me to dress to impress when I told her I was coming over to her house tonight.

We got off the bus on Damen Street looking for Greg and Jay. We spot them downtown both wearing white T-shirts and black jeans. "Guess who?" Sundae said as she came up from behind Jay, holding his eyes shut. "I hope it's the girl I've been waiting on," he said. "Hey Greg," I said with a friendly smile. He gave me a hug and asked me what took us so long to get there. I didn't even know we were coming until the last minute I told him. "Well Greg, if you must know, I had to wait before we could leave the house," Sundae said sarcastically.

We all dived into the action. There were other events going on besides the concert and downtown was pack with people. We had a great time laughing and singing songs as different artist performed on stage throughout the night. We got a picture with one of the performers and got an autograph. The next couple of days went pretty fast. I took the SAT for the first time. It's now Wednesday. I've been studying for this Spanish class for hours now and need a break.

I begin writing in my diary. Dear Diary, my boyfriend came over a few days ago and I realize I've had a change of heart and I'm no longer interested in waiting for him to leave for Carolina. He supposedly has to wait two more months before he can leave now. Some crap about his paper work missing. I put my pencil down when my mother knocked on my bedroom door. "Yes ma," I answered respectfully. My mom cracked open my door. "Hey, what are you doing? "Nothing, just writing in my journal, mom." "Writing what? "Just stuff," I said as she came and sat on the edge of my bed.

"Well Tiff, I just want you to know I had a vision the other day." "A vision of what?" I asked. "Honey, I had a vision for this family, she said with a smile. I'm telling you Tiffany, God is in this family and I can see our future with God by our side. I can't wait until we get our new house, my mother said with a smile. This family has to stick together Tiffany. Did you hear me?" "Yes Mom." "Okay I'm going let you finish writing in your journal because I have to get dinner ready." My mother then got up to leave until I interrupted her. "Ma?" "Yeah what is it?" "I love you." "I love you too," she said as she slowly closed my door. I have to find some way to fix this I said out loud to myself. The next day I got a phone call from Darius. I answered it and he sounded really excited. Hey tiff, what's up he blurted out loud on the phone. "Hey Darius where are you?" I asked? "I'm on the eastside of Atlanta," he responded. "I got some good news for you Tiffany." "What?" I asked. "Hold on Tiff."

I held on and Darius put someone on three-way with us. "Hello," the third voice inquired. "Anthony tell Tiffany that me and you solved our issues and all that stuff you told her was made up. She is on the phone right now." "Oh hey Tiff." "Hey Anthony what's going on?" I asked. "Well, yeah it's true." And that was all Anthony said before Darius hung up with him. "See baby I told you it wasn't true." "But all he said was yeah it was true," I replied. "Stop trying to make things so difficult." Then all of a sudden Darius other line began to ring and he put me on hold. He then clicked back over telling me it was his cousin and he would call me back. When I hung up the phone, it ate me up inside.

To me the way Anthony said yeah its true sounded like (I don't care if me and Darius are on good terms) I'm still telling you the truth. It was in the tone of his voice and the way he said it turned my stomach upside down. My life sounds like something from a drama book. A few days went pass and I was in the car with my mother on the way to church when she heard a familiar song on the radio. Oh yeah, this reminds of me of when I was in college my mother said with a smile. The song was "Super Star" by Luther Vandross.

My mother looked at me and then continued driving as she began telling me a story. "This girl name Laney use to be my roommate in college and she always played this song. She was in love with a boy on the baseball team. He was a big, black, country boy my mother said as she laughed." As we listened to the song, I sat in the car thinking about what I want to do with my life.

I only have five months left of high school and I have twenty-five dollars to my name. I have to get a job to pay these senior dues. The last thing I want to do is stress my mother out about money. So I never told her about the $508.00 for senior dues. Time was moving forward and Christmas break was around the corner. When it comes to Darius, I've been let down so much by broken promises that it doesn't even hurt anymore.

I called Darius cell phone and told him we need to talk. "Okay Tiff, we will talk but I'm at work so I'm ma call you back when I get off work okay." "Yeah bye," I said as I hung up the phone. It sounded like a bunch of bullshit. Darius cold blooded disappeared.

I didn't know if he was ok or if anything ever happened to him because there was no contact. Darius left me hurt to the core and angry. The next couple of weeks flew by in a breeze and there was only one week left until Christmas. After I gradually devoted my time to God my entire life began changing.

I talked to my father a few times over the phone and we were talking about me leaving for college. I can remember everything he said that day which was "you can do anything you want to do because I believe in you. I'll be here to give you what I can for your college tuition just go to school and go after your dreams."

I believe it was that day that I realized I actually love my father and everything he did in the past should stay in the past. I develop another level of maturity and learned to live in the present and not the past. People don't always stay the same and it's true that people changed. I believe you just have to be able to recognize the difference between a person who is actually changing and a person who just wants to change. For a moment, my father was there. The weekend came and my mother dropped me off downtown in front of a huge white building.

I walked into a high class restaurant looking my best of course. I came to meet Te-Te and her baby Deshon for lunch. The restaurant was very relaxing and romantic. It seems to be a place for couples rather than friends I thought to myself. I looked around and saw majority Caucasian men and women. "Excuse me Ms. Lady, what a lovely gown you are wearing. Can I help you with something?" "Yes, I'm looking for a friend of mines. Her name is Tiara and she made reservations for me to eat here tonight." "Oh you must be Tiffany." "Yes I am, I said politely." "Well, let me assist you. Ms. Tiara is at table number twenty-three." He held out his arm for me to grab so he could lead. At table twenty-three, Tiara greeted me with a quick hug and we sat down to order our food.

"Sorry I'm late girl. I was at the mall with my mom waiting on her to drop me off." "That's okay Tiffany because Carlos isn't even here yet." I was shock to hear her say those words. I stared in her eyes and but she couldn't look at me. "Oh," I replied with disappointment in my voice.

"Look Tiff," she said softly as if she was about to fix her mouth for an explanation. Carlos then interrupted by sitting down at the table with a tacky red jersey and street jeans as if he didn't care about his appearance. "Hey Te baby what's up?" "Did you tell her what I told you to say yet?" he asked her with purpose deliberation to not speak to me. "Why are you late?" Te-Te asked as if an argument was about to take place.

Carlos looked at her and smiled. "Te, I'm staying for only about ten minutes. My mom is sick and she waiting for me in the car to go to Walgreens to pick up her prescription." "If you don't believe me you can go to the car, she's out there." I hope they don't act a fool in front of these folks I thought to myself. "If she's sick Carlos then why is she waiting in the car instead staying home?" "Baby I don't want to argue. I want to take my mom to the store okay." "Te can you hurry up and just tell her?" Carlos asked as he tapped his agitated fingers on the table.

Te-Te then turned towards me. "Tiff, I asked you to come here to tell I love you and I thank you for helping me but ummmm" . . . . She hesitated but Carlos finished her words by cutting her off in a rude way. "What she trying to say is stop telling her that bull shit about me cheating and trying to break us up again." My face turned red and my insides suddenly felt hot. I decided to keep calm a tone of voice. "Out of everything you do Carlos I didn't have to try very hard now did I?"

"Look you lil heifer I'm going to be direct with you because I already don't like yo ass as it is. You think you're all that and your nothing." "Why am I nothing, because I won't allow a punk like you to hit me upside my head? I know that's what the hell you still doing to her behind closed doors you punk." It was that moment

I must have lost my temper because people in the restaurant suddenly stop eating and turned around to face our table.

Carlos then stood up at the table so I did as well. "Why don't you just leave you jealous tramp?" "You know what Carlos, you have no respect for women." I then turned to my girl who seems awfully quiet. "Come on Te-Te he hasn't change and he never will." She just looked at me as if she wish she could move but didn't. I gathered up her baby things and tried to get her to come along until she snatched the baby clothes out of my hand as if I did something wrong. "I can take care of myself Tiffany. I don't need your help she said louder than I ever heard her spoke before.

Your always trying to solve somebody else problems but you need to worry about yourself." "Bitch I almost died for you, I hollered out loud. I'm sorry but I don't risk being pulled from a 9th floor balcony unless I really care about the person, Tiara." I was deeply hurt but not surprise she chose him over me. I pick up what dignity I had left, my little black purse, and left the table. Instead of calling for a ride I decided to walk to the bus stop.

I threw my purse on the brown wooden bench and sat there looking like I just broke up with my prom date. I couldn't help but notice a car parked across the street with loud music. In the car was a light skinned girl in her early twenties sitting there as if she was waiting for someone to hop in. Ten minutes later, Carlos hoped in the car. He saw me waiting across the street and winked at me with a smile. He kissed the girl on purpose then sped off fast in his red sporty car. I was mad but there was nothing I could do.

I thought about going back in the restaurant to get Te-Te but she wouldn't believe me anyway. Exhausted I just threw my hands up in the air. "What the hell," I said out loud to myself. The situation was useless.

Exhausted, I made it home around 7pm and found a voicemail Greg left on my mother answering machine. Greg called me about a concert at 10 o'clock tonight which was just enough time to change my clothes. I really needed a lift and to just have fun so I agreed to meet him at the concert. Of course I wasn't astonished to see the phone call was a set up. Jay and Sundae was already there with Greg waiting for me. "Hey Ms. Lady, I haven't heard from you in a while. I was starting to think you didn't care." "Sorry Greg, I been a little busy going through any and everything you can imagine," I responded. Here I was at "Damen Funnel Park" at an R&B concert. Two hours later, Greg and I still haven't had any private time to talk one on one. So when Sundae and Jay ran off to get autographs, we took advantage and sat down next to the huge green waterfall. "Going through what?" Greg asked. "I know your boy hasn't been giving you problem has he?" I didn't feel comfortable going to another guy about my problems so I kept the conversation short and simple. "No, he's just acting his age," I said with a smile.

"Well as long as he don't put his hands on you is all I'm concerned about." Greg is always joking or making comments about beating up Darius I thought to myself. "I don't know what we are doing here eating ice cream in the middle of December I said," as we both laughed out loud in the cold air. There are thousands and thousands of people around us having a great time tasting weird foods from across the country. We continued to talk until Sundae came back running towards us while Jay walked behind her like he was too cool to run. "girl I got her autograph," she said excited. "Let me see," I said as I grabbed it pretending to put it in my purse. She almost tore it in half trying to snatch it back. The four of us walk towards the stage as the celebrities came out to do a few songs for the audience. It was hard trying to get clear pictures with thousands of girls going crazy. We heard every song they ever made then rushed from table to table eating sweets from over twenty seven countries.

The four of us begin to walk down Madison Street on the way home around one that morning. We missed our train so Jay and Sundae stood to the side talking as Greg and I sat on the bench waiting for the next train to arrive. "So Ms. Lady did you have a good time tonight?" "Yeah, especially when Jay wasn't paying any attention and that pole hit him in the middle of the head." "That nigga fell straight to the ground," Greg replied as we both laughed at the same time. "On the real though, Tiff, I really like you. I mean, I can't lie and say I don't."

"Greg you're a nice person but I'm just chilling by myself right now and to be honest with you I'm not so hot about you selling drugs either." Even if I wanted to jump into another relationship, selling drugs would stand in the way of me and you to be real with you. It's just something I don't want to add on to a plate full of food if you know what I mean." "It's cool then we can just hang Tiff, I love your company." The train came and the night ended with me and Sundae laughing on the way home.

Chapter Eight

Today is Monday and it's the **last week of school** before Christmas break. So many assignments, projects, and final exams can be draining. I needed to escape. So of course I went to my favorite park. It's so pretty and refreshing to be here alone. I love watching the ducks when I come here because they seem to have the perfect household. The father duck leads while the mother and children ducks swim along with him. My pastor says in church every Wednesday, "People are either bridges or blockers and there is no in between. So look at the people in your life and decided if they are blocking or bridging your life to the next level." Sitting on my favorite swing, I begin writing a poem called Ms. Number One.

It's the way I felt at the moment.

Ms. Number One

I wasn't supposed to be a victim . . . .
My life was on the right track . . . .
I guess until he came along.

I wasn't supposed to be a victim . . . .
But I loved him and gave my all . . . .
After I fell in love, it really wasn't my call.

I wasn't supposed to be a victim . . . .
But along the path I made a wrong turn
Didn't mean to get lost, but in life you live and learn.

I wasn't supposed to be a victim . . . .
So I pretended I wasn't and even moved on
But these tears never let me forget
I was his victim, **Ms. Number One**.

I left the park and headed home to finish writing on a book I been secretly working on. Christmas is now only three days away and I'm feeling good. I feel free like I've found myself again. I know one thing is true, you can't hide from God. Even when you decide not to pray, God see everything you do and no one knows your heart as he does. Right now I'm in the healing process. You know, missing that fool like crazy but at the same time getting over him. On Christmas Eve, my mother and I went to church to hear the word and I took another step in my spiritual life.

There are some things I admit I need to change about myself. Cursing is hard for me to stop since I do it on a daily basis around my friends but there are no excuses. I need to watch my words. My pastor says your tongue is a powerful possession and it does what you say. Death and Life is in the words of the tongue. So I have to be careful of the things I speak into existence. Christmas came and it was really nice. My mom loves lights and decorations so of course our house was looking like the North Pole . . . . lol.

My family called to check on us and my mother fixed a really nice dinner.

I had the best gift of the year, which was deliverance. So I can't complain about all the material things I didn't get for Christmas. Three days after Christmas, Greg gave me a call. I was in the kitchen fixing spaghetti for my baby sister when the phone rang. I have to be honest. I was hoping it was Darius. "Hello?" "Hey, Ms. Lady how are you doing?" Oh . . . . I'm fine. "That's good, you know this yo boy Greg right?" "Of course silly", I said playfully. "Greg, you know what? I was thinking about you the other day." "Oh really," he responded as if he took the comment personal. "I mean as far as you being on the streets and doing what you do." "Look shawdy, I already told you my situation and right now I'm just in some stuff I got to own up to." "Well Greg, I was thinking you could work at my job," I said happily as if I found him a solution. "Thanks lady but I'm not about to be working for eight dollars a hour when I can make three G's in one week." "I'll just hate to see you in jail one day Greg. Greg, I think you're a cool person and you just made a wrong turn. Just don't forget that you got a job when *that street thing* don't work out, okay?"

"Yeah okay, I feel you Ms. Lady . . . . Hey Tiff, Sundae told me about yo boy." "Yeah well it be like that sometimes." "Man, a girl like you, I don't know what that fool was thinking. Seriously he must have been stuck on stupid I mean you're beautiful and smart. Anyway just don't feel bad shawdy cause on the real, I'm not saying this to get with you but you're better off without him. I just didn't want to say anything when I first met you cuz I didn't want you thinking I was hating on yo boy. But on another note, I do need to get off these streets. Police is watching my every move now and just waiting for me to mess up. I'll hate for them cop suckers to get me like they got my brotha." "We'll when you ready for change Greg and just need somebody to help you with that transition then just give me call okay." "Yeah Ms. Lady, promise me you'll keep your head up and take care of yourself." "I promise, I said." Bye Tiff. Bye Greg.

When someone is ignoring you, it tends to anger that person, well me, at least. So two days later, I tried calling Darius to see if he would answer the phone but he wouldn't answer any of my phone calls. The worst part is I can't stop thinking about him and my feelings are still strong for him. I've been ignoring the situation but I got to write how I'm feeling. I opened my diary and began writing. I name the poem "subconsciously".

Subconsciously

I think I'm resting but I run **subconsciously**
This memory haunts me **daily**
Giving me the disillusion
That he's still apart of my **reality**
Then it tells me it's only my past
Therefore, I can think of it and still be **free**.
Then I have to remind it of the life and
tears it continuously steals from **me**.
So I continue on my journey
All a while subconsciously **running**
Until I'm no longer breathing
Because that's how it felt when I was **loving.**
I asked the memory if it can take these
Mental chains off of **me**
But it shy away with a mask
and doesn't answer **me**.
So I continue to search for **Mr. Remedy**

All awhile fear continue **developing**
So I stop running to **face it**
Asking it questions because I **hate it**
Then I realize this one thing is absolutely **true**
I'm still deeply in love with **you**.

Chapter Nine

It's finally the last day of the year and I admit to starting the New Year off in a childish manner. After the pain continued to sink in, I was mad as hell. I was in my room when I decided to call Darius again. I called his phone about ten times and just hung up on him. I know it was stupid but sometimes hurt people do stupid things. After the tenth time of me calling he changed his voice mail. He changed his voicemail and said you are getting this message because either A. you are boring B. You are stupid or C. you are someone I wish to not talk to right now, leave a message and I will get back to you whenever I feel like it.

I hung up the phone slamming it on the floor. I was angry and needed to think before I did something crazy. I fix something to eat and sat under a warm blanket on my couch, until my phone rang. "Hello," I answered? "Hey Tiff, what's up?" "Hey China what you been up to?" "Girl I'm up to no good, are you ready?" "Ready for what?" I asked. "Nigga don't play," she shouted playfully. "Oh yeah, I almost forgot, I said." "Yeah no doubt China but don't forget our deal. I'll help you take care of Tony's car but after that you have to help me screw up Darius car."

"Aight girl, I'm picking you this weekend Tiff." "Okay," I replied. "China, don't you have a good guy why waste time on your ex-boyfriend?" "Because the shit still hurts, even when I am dating someone else," she replied. Okay well, we in this together . . . . so "Bye Bonnie." China chuckled, "Okay, Bye Clyde." Three days later, China came to get me. I told my mother I was staying the weekend at her house and I'll be back home after school on Monday. Putting on my black jeans, I can hear China honking the horn for me to hurry up. I hopped in the car and threw a red bag on the back seat. From the looks of it, girlfriend had every tool on the floor of the passenger side.

"What's wrong Tiff, you getting cold feet girl?" "China shut up, drive this car, and we better not get caught." "Well Bonnie, I got your back and you got mines, she said." I looked over at my girl and sung out loud, I GOT YOU CLYDE, I GOT YOU BABE. She went along with the flow and sung, AND I GOT YOU BONNIE, I GOT YOU BABBBBBYYYY. China was really off beat giving us both a hard laughed.

It's two thirty in the morning and we're at Darius house. No one is here, which is working in our favor. I told China to park on the opposite side of the street. I didn't want anyone to see us.

We hop out like LAPD about to arrest America's most wanted on the side walk walking. We ran to the other side of the street dressed in black from head to toe. "Okay China, we gotta be in and out quick," I said. The first thing I grabbed from my bag was pink spray paint. I want to spray paint the name Trish permanently on the hood of his car in thick, highlighted, pink, bold letters. I figure since he likes the girl so much then he shouldn't mind seeing her name every morning.

In the middle of doing my art work, I saw China scratching the side of his car. I walk over to see what she wrote and it read "GOOD FOR NOTHING NIGGA". We both laughed. Immaturity took over and so I made a trip to the car.

I came back with eight rows of tissue and gave some to China. We threw a Halloween party over his house and car. China said it wasn't enough so she ran to the car and came back with two metal bats. "Are you crazy?" I asked while looking around to make sure no one saw her? "China someone will hear us and call the police." "It's the final touch Tiff, if you get the front then I can get the back." "Okay . . . . bet," I said. I took the bat and pictured Darius face.

I smashed in his headlights and side mirrors. China was putting in some serious dents on the back of his car. She was swinging the bat like he cheated on her instead of me. I held in a secret laugh because she was looking like one of those crazy stalking type women from t v.

People begin coming out of their houses. China and I ran to the car as fast we could. "Slow down before we get pulled over China," I said out of breath. She was driving in full speed. "Girl I can't. I don't want that woman to get my grandma's license plate number." I can't believe this fool brought out her grandmother's car I thought to myself.

"China, I thought you said this was your brother's car?" "Well, I was bringing Steeve's car but you know how he is. As soon as he gets a hot date he forgets everything he previously said." "This is moving too fast. Pull over in that parking lot until we can figure out what to do next China."

With heavy breathing, we both stepped out of the car. "So what's next?" I asked. "Are you about to pay Tony a visit, Clyde?" "Yeah that's our next bank and that's where the money is Bonnie."

"Is his money parked in front of the house?" "Naw Bonnie, I went by there before I picked you up and it's parked on the corner. We can do some serious damage." We got in the car ten minutes later and drove over to Tony's house. We damaged his car worst and spent no time doing the childish things we did with Darius car. His front and back windows was bust out. We got back in the car to pull off until China jumped out and left me inside. I couldn't see what she was doing but for the next two minutes I heard glass shattering. She came running to the car.

We got to China house four in the morning from doing our dirty work. All night we laughed and reminisce on old high school memories. China's mother was at work for the night so we played on both Darius and Tony's cell phone. We ate eat pizza and watch a movie for the rest of the night. Suddenly, China's house phone rung. China answered it but the person on the other end hung up. The caller ID said Tony Roberson.

"Girl I hope he doesn't know anything yet," China said. "You better hope not cuz if he does he gon dig in yo ass." We laughed hard then fell asleep with the red bag of crime next to us. For some reason I couldn't sleep. I tossed and turned until I finally got up.

I thought what I did would make me feel better but I knew I was wrong. Deep inside I'm hurting far more than a damage car. I got my pocket teen bible from my bag and took it to the table. I looked over my shoulder and saw China was still in a deep sleep. I looked over a few verses and couldn't help the hot tears from silently rolling down my face.

I simply read to not seek revenge on your enemies, for the Lord will take care of those who forsake you. Then I read another scripture that said I will never forsake you or leave you. I fell asleep at the table, drained. This is a heart ache I'll never in my life for forget and a lesson I will never take for granted. The weeks passed by and school continued as winter finally began to fade.

It's been three months since I've broken up with Darius and I had no idea the effect it would have on me. I've been seriously damaged. I was watching a movie one night and this lady made perfect sense. What she said made me sit back and apply her words to every area of my life. She asked you ever heard about the dog and his owner? The guy said no I don't think so.

Well, there's a country man and his dog stuck on the side of the road. A lady walks pass and see the dog moaning. So the lady asks the guy why is the dog moaning and screaming in pain. The owner says, well he is in pain because he is sitting on a nail. The lady asks why don't the dog just get up? The owner replied, I guess he's not hurting bad enough.

I must have been sitting on about five nails and it was time to get up to stop the pain. When a person is ready to move on they will get up. They would rather do whatever it takes to pick their self up rather than sit down and hurt all day.

The next day I got a phone call from an old friend. Hello, I answered. Hey Ms. Lady, how you been? Hey Greg, I'm good and what's up with you? Well actually Tiff, I was calling you to see why you haven't called a brotha in a while. No reason I guess, how you been Greg? Man, I'm straight. I've just been chilling. The phone was silent. Well, look Tiff I'll give you a call later on okay. Yeah okay Greg, I'll talk to you later. After hanging up I took off my yellow dress and threw on some slacks.

I can't believe Greg is still calling me. I was kind of hoping he wouldn't call anymore considering the last time I saw him. I'm not being shallow but truth be known, the brotha fell off bad, really bad. The last time I saw Greg was about two months ago. Sundae and I met him and his friend downtown and I couldn't believe my eyes. He was so skinny as if he lost a tremendous amount of weight. I knew it was a matter of time before something happened to him.

The street life wasn't going well for him and he lost his drug money in his house when it caught on fire three months ago. He lost so much weight that I couldn't help but to believe he was using his own product. He had that *"LOOK"* on his face when I saw him. Truth is drug dealing is a deceiving lie for quick money and it ain't for everybody. Going to jail, dying, getting beat, shot at, or having karma come back on you is too high of a price to pay if you ask me.

After seeing Greg, I made up my mind not to see him again. That's the real reason why I haven't called him. You can't change anyone who doesn't truly want to change. You'll just end up with a lot of broken expectations and wasted time. That person has to want it.

It was three in the morning when the phone begin ringing off the hook. I got up to answer it and saw Darius name on the caller id. "What's going on?" my mother screamed from her room. "I don't know," I shouted. "Hello," I answered? The other person hung up. I begin walking towards my bed but the phone rang again. "Hello," I answered. "I'm sorry Tiffany. I just had to hear your voice." "Three o'clock in the morning, Darius?" He didn't say anything. "I have to go," I said as I hung up the phone. I went back to bed but couldn't sleep. So I went to my mother's room.

I cracked the door open and could hear her sitting up in her bed. "Tiff, baby what is it?" I walked over to her speechless and she turned the light on. "Girl what's wrong with you? Why are you in here shaking? Was that Darius calling you?" "Yes mom," I replied. "I thought you told me it was over between the two of you Tiffany." "It is mom." "Well what's wrong, girl? You're in here shaking like you're going to the electric chair." "Mom, can I talk to you?" "Yeah, what is it?" "Well, I really need to tell you the truth about some stuff. Mom, I just want to move on and never look back." "Girl what are you saying?" "It's about Darius mom.

Mom I just want you to know that the next time I'm with someone the way I was with Darius, I'll be married." "Come closer Tiffany and close the door so you don't up Lacey." "I'm sorry mom. I can remember the day you told me the truth about him but I denied it." "Everything you did to separate Darius and I was to help me but I rebelled against it. I'm sorry mom, I'm so sorry." "Tiffany, the only thing that matters is that you ask the Father for forgiveness in Jesus name and then forgive Darius and forgive yourself."

"Honey, you're a young girl, so you made a young a silly mistake but always remember what doesn't kill you will always make you stronger. The most important thing about making a major mistake is learning from it so you don't have to return to it in a similar situation down the line. Remember, what you give up for the kingdom sake, God will repay you ten times and better than whatever you had to walk away from for his sake. Well Tiffany, we are going to let this night pass by and move forward in the morning. Go get some sleep. And one more thing Tiffany, always come to me when you have a problem or not sure about something. I've been your age and I been there and done that. The only thing out there that's changed since I was a teenager is the fashion. Other than that, the game remains the same and new people are born every decade to play it or either get played. I know what I'm talking Tiffany, it's just a part of growing up."

"Good night, I said as I closed her bedroom door. Christmas break has been over for some time now and there are only two months left until graduation. For spring break, my mother, sister, and I took a trip home to Detroit. We had a great family reunion. I love having family around so when we go up north, I want to see everyone. I have to be honest though. Even though the months were rolling pass, I was still angry with Darius.

I was also angry with myself because I couldn't figure out why I was continuously thinking about the boy so much. I'm ever so sure; not having any real closure with him played a major role in my pain. Church taught me how to forgive. My pastor says not forgiving someone is like swallowing poison but instead you're waiting for them to die. He says not forgiving will only hold you back not the other person. So I decided to exhale my past.

Chapter Ten

It's funny how the devil appears out of nowhere when he sees you moving forward. On a Tuesday afternoon, I decided to braid Lacey's hair in corn rolls. I hate braiding my sister's hair because she's only four and she never sits still. The phone interrupted the TV show "Barney". "Hello," I answered in a rush. "Yeah, how you been?" the voice on the other end asked.

"Who is this?" I asked. "Who you think it is?" I hung up the phone and it quickly rung again. "Hello," I answered with an aggravated voice and little patience. "Yeah, why you hang up on me?" "I don't know Darius, I guess the phone fell. I have nothing for you, what are you calling me for?" "I just want to talk to you," he replied. "No, I don't think so." "Okay, okay wait Tiff, before you hang up, what is that red thing on your head?" "What? You can see me Darius?" I looked outside my window and saw Darius and his stupid friend Mario in the car. A security guard then walked up to his car and I could hear their conversation through the phone.

"Excuse me sir, who are you hear waiting for?" the muscular looking security guard asked him. "Oh sir, I'm waiting on my girlfriend to come outside." "I'm not your girl," I said through the phone loud enough so Darius could clearly hear. "Okay, just making sure no one is here is to make any trouble the security guard said. Okay, you boys have a good afternoon." "You too sir, Darius said as the security man walked away." "Tiffany, I'm coming up to your house right now." "You got a lot of nerve to think I'm about to let you in, don't waste your time Darius." I saw Darius walking up my steps and heard him knocking at my door. He was still on the phone with me.

"Why you treating me like a stranger Tiff?" "What? You are a stranger, I said through the door." Darius then walked back to his car and drove off. "Well, I'm calling you again tomorrow Tiffany." "Don't waste your time of coming or calling me again," I said right before giving him the dial tone.

I sat back down on the couch and wrote how I felt because the tables turned. Out of my heart came a poem called **"Ancient Love"**

"**Ancient Love"**

I use to love him with
Bottomless **passion**
Titanic would've lost
against my **compulsion**

high off a drug that
Never let me **down**
like A marry go **around**
I sprung blissfully

Around and **around** . . . .
Right before I **drowned**

Suffocated with lies and
broken **promises**
Fell on top of life
long **bruises**
I finally let him go and
got rid of **excuses**.

Back again after so long
But I didn't **bother**
My love is deeper
This time
belonging to the **FATHER**.

After writing the poem, I finished up Lacey's hair. I also got a head start on my math homework. I had Kayla on the brain for some reason.

Kayla called me the other day about a having a job for me. I really wanted to know what job she was talking about because I needed money desperately to pay for my senior dues and graduation. When I called her, the phone didn't ring twice before she answered it. "Hey Tiff. I knew yo butt was gone call me." Kayla, what job are you talking about?" "First you gotta tell me what you were talking about when you told me to slow down in British Lit class on the first day of school." "Okay, Okay," I said. "Kayla everyone at the school now knows where you work at." "What are you talking about?" she asked. "Everyone knows your stripping illegally at that night club on Kelmond Street."

"Are you serious Tiff?" "YES!!!" "That's why I told you to slow down because these guys at school are talking about you." "You know what, Tiff? At the end of the day, I use to be afraid of people knowing where I work and what they will think of me and the whole nine yards. But I honestly can careless what other people think cuz I make in one hour what basic job people make in one day. Plus, don't nobody know what I go through at home and don't nobody pay me or my momma's bills, so it is what it is." Dem niggas who be talking about me can come down to the club because after they kiss my ass, I'll take their money too."

"Tiff, I'm sorry your mother lost her job but now you know what you gotta do." "Hell naw Kayla!!! No girl, I'm not stripping in NOOOO CLUB," I shouted. "Girl I already know you aint, that's not what I'm talking about. All you gotta do is become a waitress and sell the drinks there. Do a few private lap dances and that's it. You ain't gotta dance on stage or nothing. I can talk to my manager and put you on. You already know you pretty Tiffany. I promise your tips on one Saturday night will be more than what your mom use to make in two weeks. Come on Tiff, just think about it. It's not like I'm asking you to dance on stage or nothing." "I hate those kind of places Kayla. Man, my mom just got laid off. I'll think about it. I'll do it if I absolutely can't find anything else. Bye kayla."

"Okay, okay wait before you hang up . . . . How about you just come to the club tonight and I'll show you what I do. It's easy Tiffany." "So, all I'm doing is just watching?" "Yeah, just watch me until I get off work and I'll take you home." "Okay, but only tonight and what time you coming?" "I'll come to your house at 11pm." "No, you can't come here that late." "Girl, well what time you thought I was gonna come, nine in the morning? We not selling no dam cookies. This ain't girl scout Tiffany." "Okay Kayla, meet me at Sundae house." "Alright, bye Tiff."

I was just about done with Lacey's hair. I went outside to check the mailbox and couldn't believe my eyes. I planted a seed about a month ago and the fruit is now in an envelope waiting for me to open it. A month ago I applied to three different universities. I applied to a University in Florida, a college in California, and another University in North Carolina. I brought the mail inside and nervously sat at the kitchen table so I could open them. I read each letter slowly and carefully as tears of joy ran down my face. I ran to my room to call and tell my mother I was accepted in all three schools. Wow, I always knew I was going to college and now I can't wait until August of this year to start my first semester.

Later on, I went over to Sundae's house so Kayla could pick me up. She pulled up in a red Cadillac with red and black rims and tinted windows. "Hop in chick," she said smiling at me and sundae on the porch. "Call me when you on the way back Sundae," said right before she went in the house.

At 12 a.m., I saw a lot of guys drinking and loud mouthing one another in the parking lot of the club. "Girl who's truck is this?" I asked while getting out the car. Kayla laughed out loud. "Umm, it's one of my client's truck." I didn't bother to ask her any further questions. She took me to the side of the building where a guy was waiting on her to let us in. I couldn't believe my eyes. Never in my life have I seen anything like this place. The women in here are butt naked. The woman in front of me is wearing 6 inch red bottom heels with 3 huge blue star stickers covering two breast nipples and her coochie. Green glitter sparkles over her body and her long, curly, honey blonde hair falls to the middle of her back. I don't understand why a beautiful lady will dance in a place like this.

I'm sure she could get any modeling job she wanted instead of stripping. Guys were staring at her like perverts as she walk pass them. Walking fast, Kayla signals me to go into the back dressing room with her. I was right behind Kayla until I heard some strange noises. I thought I'd quickly walk five feet over and glance down the dark blue hallway. I saw a white girl sucking a black guy's dick against the wall with his hands on her head. I couldn't believe my eyes.

The guy saw me. "Unless you about to come suck my dick next get the fuck out of here," he shouted at me. Scared, I ran into the dressing room with Kayla. She was changing into her work clothes or a piece of a cloth I should say. I never saw her dress in such a provocative way.

She was wearing a leather black bra with cut out circles for nipples to hang out, a leather pink thong, a cowgirl pink and black printed hat, and black thigh high boots. "Girl what the hell you got on?" I asked her "Umm, work clothes, she answered sarcastically. "Look Tiff, this is just a job so don't take my image personal as to who I really am outside this place, Okay? You're going to see a lot of crazy shit tonight so just watch me work, have a drink or two, and relax."

"I was right behind you, how did you get dress so fast?" I asked her. "Girl, I came ready under my clothes," she replied laughing out loud. All I had on was a dress, Tiff. I just tossed it to the side." Another naked girl with nothing on but body paint of the American flag and thigh high red boots came into the dressing room. "Hey Star, I want you to meet my friend, Tiffany. You can call her Tiff"

Star came and gave me a hug. I was disgusted but didn't show it on my face. "Oh okay, Kayla this must be the girl you were talking about bringing when we talked last weekend." "Yeah this is my girl from school. Take care of her tonight. Just look after her and make sure no niggas fuck with her. It's her first night here and Star you know how it is when it's your first time stepping a foot in this crazy ass club." "Don't worry about it. I'll look after her these first few weekends until she get used to it, she said." "Ummm, excuse me Star, I won't be here but one day," I responded. Star looked into my eyes with disbelief, "Right!!!" she replied before applying lip gloss on her lips in the mirror.

Kayla walks out the room to dance and leaves me alone with Star. "So u dance or fuck?" she asks me while still pampering herself in the mirror. "Neither," I responded with a nasty tone of voice. "I'm only watching what Kayla does here and probably just serve a few drinks, that's it." Star laughed as if she heard the joke of the year. "Girl that's what we all say on our first night here. Believe it or not you'll start dancing up and down that pole just like the rest of em hoes. All you gotta see is a couple of hundred dollar bills and yo mind gon change real quick."

"I doubt it, I respond with an attitude." "Tiff, I can already see you a snobby one. Im ma have to break you in with yo stubborn acting ass," she says as she open the dressing room door. She then led me to a table on the dance floor. "Stay here Tiff, Im ma get you a drink. Don't talk to strangers," she said sarcastically.

I waited uncomfortably for Star to return. Finally, She hands me a blue drink. It smells like liquor and some kind of berry. "Dam girl it's just a little liquor, gone and drink it. I aint gon do you wrong," she said. "Yo stuck up ass need to relax if you gon make it up in here. Kayla says she know you from school. Well, honey, this a different type of class room." I took a sip and surprisingly it was sweet. I easily drunk the drink and about ten minutes later Star gave me another one. "Star, I don't want to get drunk." "Honey this is only your second drink. Relax, so you can make some money tonight. Now drink this one a little slower because it's stronger."

Even though there was ice in the drink, a burning hot sensation was streaming down my throat. I reach for my neck and began coughing. "Girl I told you to take it easy. Here's some water. Make sure you drink the entire cup of water. You see that guy tipping that stripper over there in the red shirt, Tiff?" "Yeah I see him." "Okay, Im ma let you have him tonight. He's usually my regular. That nigga comes here 4 times a week to see this phat ass." "That mutha fucka got money." Star lit a blunt and passed it to me. "I'm good Star, I said as I push her hand away. "Look, gon to the bar and get him his regular. He gets vodka with a splash of strawberry. That's his favorite and that's also your first ten dollars."

I did as she told me. When I got to his table, he grabbed his drink without saying a word to me. He then put ten dollars in the band around my thigh. I looked up towards the bar area and saw Star smiling at me when she saw the money. This is easy, I thought. The night was moving fast. Towards the middle of the night, I stepped to the side and counted four hundred and twenty-three dollars from just serving drinks throughout the night. The guys were drunk and tipped me every time. Kayla checked on me twice then went back to the dance floor.

The last customer I served was a guy in his mid-30s'. He was with two of his friends at a table drinking and receiving lap dances from other working girls. I gave him a shot of tequila. He put a hundred dollar bill in my band. When I tried walking off he grabbed my hand and asked for a dance. "I'm sorry, I don't dance." "Do you see that hundred dollar bill I put on your thigh?" he asked me. "Yes and thank you but I don't dance," I responded. As I turn around to walk off, he slaps me on the ass.

"No worries, I'll break that new piece of ass in real soon," he said loud and confidently.

I turned around with rage and anger in my eyes. Before I could open my mouth, Star grabs my arm with force and pushes me to walk with her. "Tiffany, did you get money from him?" "Yes I did but he" . . . . "But nothing Tiff, just keep it moving because you want his money again the next time he comes. That guy comes and tips hundred dollars bills every time he comes. Don't let his comments get to you. You're going to hear a whole lot of comments from different niggas but it don't mean shit just ignore them and keep collecting that money. As long as a nigga stay in his seat and don't force you to go outside don't worry about it."

"Bitch your too uptight come to the bar and drink this last drink with me," she said with a smile on her face. "Im ma make you feel better okay." Whatever Star gave me before taste similar to the last drink she gave me. After the last drink, I was able to do 2 more tables before everyone around me began sounding louder and louder. The music sounded off beat. The girls on stage were all dancing slow at the same pace. The lights in the club turned dark red.

People who were on the other side of the club seem to be very close. I'm feeling sluggish and tired. I decide to lay my head down on a table to stop the dizziness. Waking up, not realizing I fell asleep, I can feel something wet going up and down my private parts. My eyes are extremely heavy as if my eye lids are paralyzed. I'm conscious, I can feel and I can hear, but I can't see. Something is on my mouth. Something very tight is on my feet and hands.

I'm hearing someone else here with me. I'm scared as hell, I can't see anything. What is this guy doing to me. I've been drugged. I need Kayla. Where is Kayla? I screamed her name but nothing but quiet muffles is what I hear coming from myself. This wet object is going up and down on my private part. It's now moving faster. Shamefully, it feels good. I feel violated with no control. I don't want this to feel good. This is rape.

This must be a tongue. His tongue is now flickering back and forth over my clitoris. It feels good. I can't remain silent any longer. Shamefully, I can't help but moan as he moves his tongue faster in circular motions. My breathing is heavy and I'm feeling something I've never felt before. My body has now watered as he continues licking me. I then heard her laugh.

This is not a man, it's a female!!! "Your eyes are close but I wish you could see your face, she says to me." It's Star I'm hearing!!! I can hear Star's voice, I thought to myself. "Why you looking like that? You sexy bitch." "I wanted to lick yo shit as soon as I seen yo ass," she said.

Feeling shame, I decided not to respond to her. "You'll be okay. I'm ma stay here with you until that pill wear off." I then heard someone bust open the door with a strong force. "Get the fuck off my friend" Kayla's angry voice shouted loudly. I then blacked out again.

The next time I woke up, Kayla was staring at me. I looked at her without saying a word. "Tiffany, You okay?" "Yeah," I responded while looking around. I feel a sense of relief knowing I'm in her room. I'm not sure how or when we left the club but I'm happy the night is over. I can see a weird pain in Kayla's eyes as if she regrets taking me to her job. "Tiff, are you sure you're okay? How does your body feel?" "I'm fine Kayla" "Girl I was so scared because I didn't know what Star gave you." "I thought I was going to have to take you to the hospital." "I'm so sorry Tiffany."

"I knew Star liked girls but not for a second did I think Star would try you like that. She looked out for me when I first started dancing at the club so I thought she would do the same for you. That girl has changed though. She's been getting wild ever since she's been popping those molly's.

"Tiff, do you wanna talk about it? "Kayla, let's just talk about it tomorrow. I honestly don't know what I'm feeling right now. I'm actually confused," I said as I turned over in her bed and pulled the covers over my head. "Okay, sleep in my bed Tiff, Im ma sleep on the couch and I'll take you home tomorrow but we got to talk before you leave." Kayla left the room with the door open.

That night, I tried going to sleep but heavy breathing and cold sweats kept waking me up. A secret I have absolutely not told anyone about is this nightmare I've had off and on for almost a year now. I don't know why I continue to have this dream. I looked around Kayla's room and found a pen and some paper. I decided to write down the dream to see if I can comprehend what's going on in this dream and what it really means.

Dear Diary,

This dream consists of me running from a non-human living presence I can't see but feel. After having this dream several times, I believe it's symbolic for something currently existing in my life. This dream comes repetitiously over and over again no matter how late or early I go to bed. I now understand I'm not running from an external man but my internal self.

When I go to sleep, I find myself on harsh streets at night time. I look around and it seems as if I'm the only person alive on earth. Even though it's night, the weather is not hot or cold. Instead, it feels as if it doesn't exit. No cars are seen on the street and every public business is close. There are no people or animals to be found for as far as I can see.

As soon as I turn to my right I can feel this strong hateful presence of something or someone. This unknown presence is very powerful and fear sits in my body. My intuition tells me the unknown presence was designed to kill me. As the presences get closer, my heart beats so hard and fast that it gives me a rhythm to run with. My mind is telling me to run faster or die. I begin running until I find a building with an open door. I go into the brick building for safety but the unknown presence is still able to imprison me if I don't continue to run.

I run through this empty school looking building and turn into an extremely long hallway. The hallway has four red doors and I'm struggling with anxiety to open each door but only the last door on the end of the hallway will let me through. The unknown presence seems to move faster now that I found an open door.

I run faster due to fear but the door that let me through leads me to another hallway with twice as many doors, making me feel hopeless. Once again, all the red doors are locked until I reach the very last one and open it.

This time the door leads me to a staircase that leads me to a room with no doors to escape from just a window. I have nowhere to run and the unknown presence is so close I feel as if I'm about to die. I then look at the window and can look down over tremendously tall buildings. I then debate on taking my life or let the unknown presence kill me. I jump to my death and can feel myself falling. I've gotten use to killing myself in the dream with the knowledge of knowing I'll wake up if I just jump.

I had the dream so many times that I began to feel laugher around me as if I've been through the procedure too many times. I would have the same dream ever so often but the *Very Last Time Had A Different Ending.*

Dear Diary, tonight this nightmare ended differently.

When I opened the last red door in the hallway, it lead me a room without windows but with a huge red door bigger than I ever seen it before. Due to fear I ran to it as fast as I could, hoping to escape the unknown spirit. This particular red door was made of strong metal and consists of several locks from top to bottom. I rush to unlock all the locks and as I was unlocking it, I felt as if the unknown spirit slowed down on chasing me. The very last lock was too high for me to reach so I got a foot stool from the corner of the room to unlock it. When I finally opened the door I saw a light too bright for my eyes and I immediately woke up.

Diary,

I don't take repetitious dreams for granted. The dream has strong meaning but even to this day, I'm still not sure of its direct essence towards me. I can only write the dream on paper and make assumptions such as it was a message from God.

After writing everything down, I look over to see 6:34 a.m. I threw on one of Kayla's sweat shirts and a pair of jeans. I quietly slid out the front door and went to my favorite park. I then wrote this poem out of frustration called **"Repetition"** because it was in my heart.

Repetition

And around I go and around I go.

I'm on the battle field
of living my **life**
So many decisions
lurking the **sky**
everytime I take one

negatively
it gets my life so very **high**
I'm wrong
whether I turn left or **right**
I'm tired
whether I sleep or **not**
It's like, what's next?
My soul is already up for **option**
It got lost in the twist of **repetition**
It's been gone so long
don't blame me I didn't know it was **missing**
It's like a **separation**
so I retaliated by **running**
It's too hard to face
But At the end of the **day**
I get on my heavenly knees and
I began to **pray**.
Now I lay me
down to **sleep**
I pray the LORD my
soul to **keep**
If I should die
before I **awake**
I pray the LORD
my soul to **take**
Amen
Amen? Amen? **Amen?**
Naw, not amen??
Not in my world, it's never **end**
Instead, I have night mares
and that same song **begins.**

And around I go and around I go

In my dreams I'm being **chased**
Then I wake up and realize
It's the way I been living these last **days**
I'm living like I'm Muhammad **Ali**
But without GOD
Just like Mike Tyson
My voice **squeaks**
You see I'm hiking
I'm on a life mission
Steady by the day
Searching for
Ms. Lady **Liberty**
To stop these issues
From smothering **me**
Fear made **Mr. Remedy**
Up and abandoned **me**
Because he was too
afraid to pull me out
Of this masquerade of **insanity**
So twisted, I wonder
what the hell is going to **save me**
So sick of running
I surrender because
These circles are making a fool of **me**.
I'm playing this game wondering if it's really **real**
habit actions are misleading me
to believe this is how I **feel**.
I know in my heart false
Prophecy fades **eventually**

So why am I internally **killing me?**
Procrastinating the growth
Of my potential **reality**
when all said and done
Only the LORD son
JESUS the savior
Can save me.

I then took a moment to look at such a beautiful lake. I remember telling China how grateful I was of God's forgiveness even though I feel like I don't deserve it. She then told me she wrote a poem similar to our conversation and she wanted me to have it. It's been folded in wallet ever since. It's called *"Your Grace, Your Ways"*

Your Grace, Your Ways

When I think of your
Your grace, your ways
I cry cuz you loved ***me***
Your grace, your ways
Loved me through my **sin**
Your grace, your ways,
Forgives the iniquity **within**
No limitations, **discrimination,**
Or **retaliation**
Even after I brought you
Humiliation
By not loving myself
Playing wife but in reality
Self Degrading

I cry cuz you loved me
In the pool of
Self pity
Position of a queen
You still place **me**
I cry cuz you loved me
Your grace, your ways
Loved me through my **sin**
Your grace, your ways
Forgives the iniquity **within**
Challenging the inner being
of **me**
Demanding the greater of me
Wins **victory**
And I cry
cuz through it all
Lord, **you still loved me.**

I like the poem China wrote. It's one of my favorites.

Chapter Eleven

This is the last month before graduation. It's now May and the book I've been writing is finally ready to be published. Graduation is only three weeks away and the senior class trip is even closer. I'm so excited to go to Mexico with my girls and have a great time. Everyone has their passports and clothes ready for the trip. Tonight Sundae and I are at Java Monkey. It's one of my favorite poetry spots downtown on Ashborn Avenue.

Sundae insisted I need to get out the house tonight. The girl signed me up on a list to perform. I didn't know it until I heard my name. The man on the microphone called Ms. Unique to the stage. I got up and recited a poem I had on my heart for over a week. "Hello everyone. I don't have a story to entertain you with so I'm ma just jump into a short poem I wrote a week ago." It's called "My Unquenchable Spirit".

My Unquenchable Spirit

I'm ready to grow up
From my childish ways
Saying hello to paradise
And goodbye to old days
I'm looking for a better language
Called communication
Giving up fornication
My generation will be
A better organization
Getting rid of societal disputation
No longer
each other's imitation
Be original
or sink in disqualification
My feet are stable
leaving the strongest
man cripple and disable
As far as my memory
I'm only here because of God's mercy
His bible is not a mystery
But should be taken seriously
Whether you're Muslim, Baptist, or Methodist
Just listen to this
And if you still can't comprehend
The meaning of these words
Just remember a strong woman of
God was the voice you heard.

My peers applauded and I left Sundae inside of Java Monkey shortly after.

Chapter Twelve

Sundae, you're a fool but I love you." "Tiff, I'm not kidding." "Okay so you're telling me that you looooovvveeee me sooooo much that you followed Darius in your car to spy on him?" "Yes bitch and listen to me cuz what I'm saying is the truth and I'm not joking" "Okay what's up?" "Tiffany, Darius was one hundred and ten percent cheating when ya'll was together." "So, why you telling me this now Kayla? You should have told me this months ago when it mattered." "I didn't say anything because your stubborn ass cut me off when I tried time ago." "Look, just listen to the story cuz its real.

"You my girl and I was tried of the bullshit so I followed him after he called you and said he was at his mom house. And yes he was at his mom house because when I got there his car was parked out front. About 10 mins later I saw him leaving the house so I followed him. He made a really quick stop at this abandon looking house on the corner from where he stay." "Yeah the red house. Darius says his cousin lives there, I said." "Girlfriend unless his cousin's first name is crack and last name is house, he's a lie."

"Are you serious?" "Seriuos as a heart attack. He wasn't there no more than 5 mins. He sells drugs tiffany. He got in the car and sped off in a rush. I stayed behind him until he pulled up to this yellow brick house.

Before he could even get out the car a girl came outside like she was expecting him and gave him a hug. Tiff, the girl grabbed his crotch and they walked into the house. The lights in the house never came on. I tried my best to wait it out but I got sooooo sleepy. So I went home and set my alarm clock for 6am. My gut feeling told me to go back and see if he was still there.

I got there around 6:30 am and I swear it was meant for me to see them cuz they came out as soon as I park my car." "So how did they not see you?" I asked. "Girl you know im not a fool. I was parked on the other side of the street but I saw everything at an angle. They came out on the porch and the girl was kissing Darius in his mouth. Then she went in the house but Tiff I didn't tell you the worst part." "What?" I asked. "Kayla paused on the phone. The girl is pregnant." "What?" "Like you could see that she's showing?" "Yes, she's at least 5 months. I couldn't see her during night but it was clearly visible during day.

Even though me and Darius is not together, heavy tears began welling in my eyes. "Are you fucking serious Sundae?" Before Sundae could answer me I turned the corner and saw Lacey swinging back and forth a long piece of metal as she sung along with Barney infront of the tv.

I looked closer and couldn't believe my eyes. Lacey had a gun in her hand. Instantly a shock came over my entire body from top to bottom. I was scared but didn't want to scare her by hollering. I didn't want her to get excited and accidently pull the trigger.

I trembled as I starred at her with heavy eyes. In a calm and shaky voice I called her name. "Lacey honey, stop jumping and turn around okay?" Lacey turned around aimlessly pointing the gun at me as she continued singing her happy song with the gun in her hands.

"Yeah, yeah, yeah, rain drops, rains drops, rain drops, go down, down, down." "Lacey honey, can you please put the toy down." "Me hungry Tiffey." Lacey then put the gun in her mouth treating it as a chewing toy. I felt like I was going to faint and couldn't hold myself together anymore.

I screamed and with every force in my body ran toward my 3 year old baby sister but she got scared and the gun went off. I saw a piece of her head fly across the room. My body collaspse to the floor with Lacey in my arms. The blood continously came from the back of her head. I could feel her take her last breath and watched her eyes rolled to the back of her head. I've never felt a pain so strong that it felt physical. I cried so hard and held her tight. I suddenly felt a hard lump in my throat and threw up on the side of her.

I ran to the end of hallway to grab the house phone. I put 911 on speaker phone and ran back to Lacey. "911, what's your emergency?" "My address is 3566 Oatlanen Street, my baby sister is dead. The gun went off in her mouth. Can u please send someone, I hollered fast with fear." "Okay, you have to slow down so I can hear your address again. Caller, did you hear me? I need you to say your address again. Hello? Are you there? I need to hear your addressed again."

I heard the dispatcher on speaker phone but my body and voice was nonresponsive. I couldn't move another inch or say another word as I stared at my sister's tiny hands. I notice the tips of her fingers were turning blue. When the police arrived, they had no other choice than to kick down the door. I was unable to let go of Lacey's body to open it.

I screamed as they tried to help me by taking Lacey's body to the hospital. I knew that moment was the last moment I'll ever see her nearly alive. I was at the kitchen table answering questions from an investagor and another cop until I saw two more cops enter into my kitchen.

The questions change from asking me what happened and into suspicious questions of me being Lacey's killer. I told them I had no idea where the gun came from and said it could possibly be my boyfriend's because he is the only person I ever allowed to come over. I told them we were no longer dating and I'm assuming he left a gun at my house. They told me to go get his phone number.

I knew then they were going to arrest me regardless If I got the number or not. When I went to my room I closed the door and threw my bloody shirt on the floor. In thirty seconds, I threw on something clean, snatched my money from my mattress, grabbed my ID, cell phone and charger, then climbed out of my bedroom side window.

I ran as fast as I could through the woods facing the back of the apartment building. Periodically, I looked back and saw more police cars pulling up to my mother's apartment. As I ran, I called a cab to meet me a mile down the street at a gas station. When I got there, the cab was waiting. I hop in and told him to take me to a motel on the out skirts of downtown called "Rains Motel". This particular motel has been known for prostitution and homeless people renting and living. I knew it was dangerous but I also knew I would be safe from the cops.

I paid for two nights and stayed in the room without eating for two days. I was trying to figure out what the hell was going on. I tried to figure out where the gun came from and why was it in my house. I felt like I was set up. It had to be Darius, I told myself out loud. If its his gun then that means his ass either got a copy of my key to the apartment or was planning to come back while I was there to get it. That might explain why his ass came over with his friend Mark in the car but couldn't get in.

The second day of staying at the hotel, I woke up to a loud noise outside. Out of my window I could see cops down stairs entering the motel towards the front entrance. They were there for a long time until I saw the owner come out with the third cop answering all his questions.

The police officer went to his car and slowly drove off as the chunkie owner stood outside watching his car drive far down the street. Suddenly, with urgency, he walked up the stairs to the floor I was on. I heard a loud knock on my door. I open it. "Hey, I don't know what the hell you got going on with the police but you gotta get the hell out of here. I got enough trouble with people in this motel. The only reason I didn't tell him you were staying here is because they're already trying to shut my motel down and giving a room to a fugitive just might get the job done. Look, you got ten mins to get out. Leave that room key on the bed."

"Okay sir, I understand," I said as I slowly closed the door in his face. I packed the one bag I had and left the room in less than five mins. I couldn't be seen in daylight so I stood near the back of the hotel building until a cab came and got me. I had him drop me off at my favorite park. I felt like I was loosing my mind and that was the only place I could momentarily become sane.

I turned on my phone and saw over 72 missed calls from my mother and 39 missed calls from Sundae. Plus a bunch of random miss calls from different numbers I've never seen before. I was ever so sure my mother's phone was tap so I took a risk texting Sundae instead.

"Hey Sundae tell my mother I love her. I would never hurt Lacey and tell her im okay." I knew the police would track me down at the park in a matter of mins if I kept the phone on me. So after my last text, I immediately threw my phone in the lake and left the park. The rest of the night I hid in another low budget hotel. I stayed out of the public so I could get my thoughts together. Now that I remember, my friend did tell me over the phone that Darius was selling drugs. I just forgot about it when I saw Lacey with the gun her hands.

This is so fucked up. Everything makes sense now. Even Anthony told me Darius real name on the street was JoJo. Darius lived a double life and when things couldn't stay separated thats when our relationship began going down hill. I'm assuming this bitch must have hid his gun in my house along with some other stuff I have no idea about. I never did go to sleep. Instead, the sun set and rose as I sat up in bed wide awake with my back against the wall thinking to myself. I can't sleep because I know I'll have nightmares of Lacey's blood all over my body again.

It's been six days now. I don't know if I'm in trouble, going to jail, or just made this situation hard on myself. I just know im hurting for my baby sister and I'm scared at the same time. With absoultely no money to my name, I decided to spend the last night under a bridge before going home. I was force to leave the hotel room in the morning during check out time yesterday. Today, Ive been walking around thinking, crying, and talking to myself outloud as people near me just looked at me. I assume they think I'm crazy but I could care less. This entire situation has happened so fast that it seems unreal. My sister isnt dead, I'm not a runaway, and darius is not a drug dealer who lived a double life and set me up. Should I kill myself? Naw, that's what the devil wants me to do.

I really feel like I'm loosing it. For the past six days I've had a thousand thoughts dominating my mind. It's still spring so the nights are still chilly. Tonight I'm sitting here alone under this bridge. It's 10:37 p.m. and I can't even think to close my eyes. I never knew what homeless people went through.

I can only imagine because I feel so vulnerable right now. I feel like I can't lay down on this ground because I have no idea what will be in my face when I wake up. This is torture. It's so nasty under this bridge. I can't stop these tears from falling. When I go home in the morning, Ill have to face whatever it is that life is going to throw at me. So emotionally unstable right. I wish I could get my body to stop shaking.

Looking at my watch its only 3 a.m. This is truly the longest night of my life. Mentallly drained and deranged, there is only one thing left for me to do. I have no one and nothing to lean on right now but God. **So I got on my hands and knees to pray.**

God, I'm in alot of trouble and I'm not sure what is going on. I'm so hurt right now about Lacey and I just pray you guide me and somehow give me peace as I return home. I pray that the truth comes out because I don't want to go to jail or have any charges of Lacey's death on me God. I know I was wrong for running away from the police and its probably a charge for doing so but I pray Father, that you have mercy on me. I'm scared God. Please give me strength. I got off my knees, wiped my tears, and began walking home. I got home three hours later at 6 a.m. I rang my mother's door bell. She finally answered the fourth time I rung it.

"Where the hell you been?" she asks me as she held me tight. "I'm sorry mom. I didn't know what to do." "Get in here, she said as she pulled my arm inside the

house." I notice everything in the house was packed up in boxes. "Mom is the poilce looking for me?" "No, if you would have answered my calls, I could have told you that. They investigated the prints on the gun and traced it back to Darius. All they wanted from you was information Tiffany."

My mother went into the kitchen then handed me the phone to call darius. "Darius has no idea Lacey is dead but he does know the police is looking for him because he is hiding out," my mother said. "Call him now Tiffany on this house phone while I call the police to get over here." "Mom, what make you think he's going to come over here?"

My mother then stormed out of the room and quickly came back with a black bag. "His ass gon come back for this." "What's in the bag?" "Tiffany, Darius left seventeen thousand dollars." "Ma, the police didn't see this when they search over this house?" "The money was in the wall behind a picture, Tiffany. What I would like to know is when did this mutha fuckha have enough time to dig a hole in my dam wall and put seventeen thousand dollars in it? Don't answer that question just call his ass over here."

I called darius over and he obviously agreed to come because of the money he thought I had no idea about. I heard knocks at the door an hour later. I opened it and immediately saw police from afar walking up towards Darius who is still unaware. I looked him in his face with anger. "Whats up, Tiff?" "Can, I come in so we can talk right quick?" "No," I responded as I pushed him away from entering the door. "Right here is fine.""Lacey found

your gun and because of your inconsiderate stupid ass she shot herself dead.

The look on darius face was priceless. Before he could say a word two officiers turned him around. "Are your Darius Cornish?" "Yes, I am." "Your under arrest for Burglary, the death of Junior Harris, drug trafficking, identity theft, attempted murder, and negligence discharge of a firearm.

"You have the right to remain silent. Anything you say can and will be used against you in a court of law. You have the right to an attorney. If you cannot afford an attorney, one will be provided for you. Do you understand the rights I have just read to you?"

"Man back the hell up off me. Back the hell up off me man," Darius hollers as he struggles to get his hands free. I watch darius as they walk him over to the police car. "Tiff, Tiff, tell them it aint my gun tiff." I just looked at him with a cold face. "Tiff, please tiff tell them its not mine."

The officer then pushed his head in the back seat of the car. My mother stood by my side as the police car drove down the street. Once the police car was out of site, my mother turn towards me and slap my face so hard I can taste the blood from inside my mouth. "I know it's not your fault why Lacey is dead but the situation could have been avoided if you would have stop dating that low life darius a year ago."

She then went into the house and cried so loud I could hear her from outside. The guilt sank in my body knowing I played apart in Lacey's death by dating someone I was told not to but by no means would I have allowed darius to hide a gun in my house or danger my sister knowing it. I felt like the situation was a no win. Darius goes to jail, I have to live with this guilt in my heart, my sister is dead, and my mother is deeply grieving. I went to my room and tried to sleep off the nightmare.

The next day was a reality check. It no longer felt like a dream, it was real. My friends and classmates went to the senior trip to Mexico and will be back tomorrow, the day before graduation.

I grieved for the next 24 hours. My mother and I both ignored family and friends phone calls. So tired of the phone ringing, I answered it. It was Kayla asking to meet me at Piedmont park. To keep my sanity, I had to get out the house so I agreed to see her.

I spotted Kayla from a far at the edge of the lake feeding the ducks. I went over and tapped her on her shoulder. She turned around and hugged me. "Hey hon, it feels great out here" she said, glancing up at the sky. I'm so sorry about Lacey, Tiff." "Let's go sit in the shade under that tree over there girl." We walked over, sat down, and Kayla's face grew sadder and sadder.

"What's wrong Kayla?" "Tiff, I never apologize to you about what happened at the club" she said, apologetically." "I just wanted to tell you I'm so sorry." "Kayla it's not your fault, you're not the one who did it to me." "Yeah but I put you in that environment Tiff." "You know what Kayla, since Lacey, I realized we live and we learn. Life is too short to be mad at somebody and I don't have angry feelings towards you. Since my sister's death I've been doing a lot of thinking. Small mistakes don't matter anymore it's all about moving forward with life."

"Thanks Tiffany, I really needed to hear that. I quit the club by the way." "Good, that place was changing you for the worst anyway. That's why I told you at the beginning of the school year to slow down. "Tiffany, I honestly lost my virginity when I was 13 years old." After that situation I thought I may as well have sex because I'll never be perfect anymore. I now realize one mistake doesn't have to be the rest of your life. I just want to say thank you

Tiffany. I mean I know you're not perfect but your relationship with God and your determination to be better has truly changed me to be a better person. I think highly of myself now. I just have to say thank you from my heart, Tiff"

Kayla reached into her pocket. I got something I want you to read. "What is it?" I asked. She hands over a piece of paper folded in half. "Tiffany, I like the way you write down your ideas to express yourself so I figured I'd write a poem. I named it "Sweet Thirteen," she said.

"Tiffany, this poem is what I wish someone would have written for me when I was 13 so I could understand my value better. This poem is for every 13 year old lil girl out there to prevent them from going in the wrong direction. I gotta go Tiff. I'll see you at graduation." "Okay Kayla." "I love you Tiff." "I love you too Kayla."

I watched Kayla run away, then looked down at the yellow piece of paper. I read it out loud.

"Sweet Thirteen"

When you have sex
What are you looking for?
Are you trying to keep him?
If so, leave him!
Are you lost?
Maybe it's because
You don't know your cost.
So what are you doing?
Besides giving and using yourself,
If he cared, he wouldn't play with you
Then put you on a shelf.

So what are you doing Miss. Thirteen?
Besides losing your soul,
steady ignoring God,
your heart is growing cold.
So what are you trying to do?
Compete with the girl next to you?
(The one without morals)
Are you trying to compete with the attention?
The kind guys are giving her for only a minute?
Then toss her to the side saying I hit it?
Are you after love?
Because your value, you're unaware of?
Is sex so important that you can't
look beyond it to see your dreams.
Is it true that sex is love and love is
Sex and that's what it truly means?
Are you running but searching for
Answers at the same time?
Questions your father never gave you because
He was too quick to leave yo ass behind?
Is it worth having a baby, who'll put
your childhood to an end?
Then once the baby grows up, do what?
Do it all over again?
Is life repetition?
Should you get involved because the
girl next to you using her sex
is considered your competition?
There are some things
Ladies don't understand.
Why give your man what's

worth giving your husband?
How can you say your man is your future
Husband or even compare the two
When your man doesn't belong to you?
Once again Miss thirteen
What are you doing it for?
Can you spell the word love out of sex?
What's between your legs
That's so different then the next?
Nothing,
but you could use your mind for
something!!!

By the time I reached the end of poem, tears were falling down my face. I've known Kayla for 6 years now and I never seen this side of her. I never knew she was watching me and listening to my feelings about God because she seemed uninterested about God. I'm touched that I had an influence on her. So now I wonder how big of an influence I'd have on people if I truly pursue God with all my heart and kick out the distractions.

Chapter Thirteen

Today is finally graduation. I'm currently standing in line with Te-Te, Kayla, Sundae, and China waiting for our names to be called upon stage to receive an award worth four years of our lives. I looked over in the audienece and saw my mother in the front row crying and smiling at the same time. I then saw Kayla and Sundae's mother sitting next to each another. Finally, I saw Te-Te's mother and her baby sitting alone. There was absolutely no Carlos insight which made me smile.

We received our awards and listened to our senior president make a speech. Suddenly I heard my name. "Welcome to the stage Tiffany Johnson" My peers applauded as I confusingly approach the stage. "Tiffany, I'm amazed that you're here at graduation after a major loss in your family. Your friend Tiara says you write poetry and I'd like you to speak from your heart. "Okay," I said.

Ummmm . . . this poem is called ***"Never Settle"***

<u>"Never Settle"</u>

Lesson one,
Never settle for **<u>less</u>**
No compromising,
Second guessing,
Nothing but the **<u>best</u>**
Set high expectations
And follow them **<u>through</u>**
No one possess the power
To stop them
Unless it's **<u>you</u>**
The sun goes up
Then **<u>down</u>**
Take responsibility
Get your butt off the **<u>ground</u>**
I'll keep my head to the **<u>sky</u>**
Until the day I **<u>die</u>**
Never asking **<u>why</u>**
Stepping on negative situations
To help me **<u>fly</u>**
Never second guessing the **<u>past</u>**
If it's not here
It wasn't meant to **<u>last</u>**
As I walk the earth
I'm **<u>blessed</u>**
I'm super woman
<u>With bullet-proof vest.</u>

Chapter Fourteen

It's the day after graduation and Ive been packing boxes all day and cleaning out my room. Out of the three letters I receive from school, I decided to go to school in North Carolina. I've been reminiscing on the good and bad times I've had this year with my friends. We are absolutely not the same girls we were before our senior year of high school but that's truly a good thing. We have grown in many ways and learned lessons. Some lessons harder than others but they allowed us to grow into stronger beings. I figure I'd write one last poem in my dairy. So I wrote what was in my heart.

I named it **"Walk It Out"**

Walk It Out

War on the battle field
Fighting the **unknown**
No longer singing the
same old **song**

but
thirsty to bring destiny **home**
my life is rolling
with wheels **on it**
thrilled to see the next scene
for a long time
I been searching **for it**
It's here, all I gotta
Do is **take**
Stay strong, **don't brake**
Seek the opportunity
It's given to **me**
A gift from ms. Liberty
Cuz I chased everything
Coming to **me**
Sacrificed the **rest**
To conquer and gain the **best**
Destroyed is **restored**
Prosperity and authority
Welcome aboard
It was only a matter of **time**
I'm taking back what
the hell is **mine**
let this big light **shine**
It's time to **grin**
Taking everything
you said
I couldn't **have**
Same mission, **different path**
I'm not winning
I won

I'm not succeeding
I'm successful
I'm not **lost**
My price was paid upon a **cross**
I'm on a predestined **route**
With army boots
It's time to walk it out.

Chapter Fifteen

Dear God, ...

. . . . thank you!

Chapter Silly Sixteen

My mother is finally moving into her house the same day I'm leaving for college. My book actually came in the mail this morning. I swear it couldn't have had better timing to get here. I put my last bag in the car and just looked at the old apartment. I have overcome so many things this year. I was having sex with my boyfriend not because I wanted to but because I believed if I didn't then he would do it with someone else.

I struggled with low self esteem but it feel great to be empowered at this moment knowing I have over come silliness and I don't have to accept it ever again. I learned life is truly short and its not a guarantee you'll live long just because your young. My sister is an example of that. Even though I'm not perfect, I learned to go to God for everything because he wants nothing but the best for me. God pre-destined a perfect life for me before I was born. The only reason I wasn't living it is because I didn't believe it. I put on my shades, start the ignition, then hit the express for North Carolina. I'll never be silly again.